REQUIEM

ALSO BY ANTONIO TABUCCHI

Letter from Casablanca
(Translated by Janice M. Thresher)

Little Misunderstandings of No Importance
(Translated by Frances Frenaye)

Indian Nocturne
(Translated by Tim Parks)

The Edge of the Horizon
(Translated by Tim Parks)

Pereira Declares
(Translated by J. C. Patrick)

The Missing Head of Damasceno Monteiro
(Translated by J. C. Patrick)

ANTONIO TABUCCHI

REQUIEM

A HALLUCINATION

TRANSLATED FROM THE PORTUGUESE
BY MARGARET JULL COSTA

A NEW DIRECTIONS BOOK

Originally published as Requiem by Quetzal Editores, Lisbon, in 1991. This translation is
published by arrangement with Harvill, an imprint of HarperCollinsPublishers, Ltd.,
London. The "Note on Recipes" at the end of the book is reprinted by courtesy of Giangia-
como Feltrinelli Editore, © Feltrinelli 1992.

Manufactured in the United States of America
New Directions Books are printed on acid-free paper.
First published clothbound by New Directions in 1994
and as NDPaperbook 944 in 2002
Published simultaneously in Canada by Penguin Books Canada Limited

Library of Congress Cataloging in Publication Data
Tabucchi, Antonio, 1943–
    Requiem: a hallucination / Antonio Tabucchi ; translated from the Portuguese by
Margaret Jull Costa
    p.   cm.
    ISBN 0-8112-1270-X (alk. paper)
    I. Title.
PQ4880.A24R46165   1994   93-46672
869.3'42—dc20   CIP

New Directions Books are published for James Laughlin
by New Directions Publishing Corporation,
80 Eighth Avenue, New York 10011

NOTE

THIS STORY, which takes place on a Sunday in July in a hot, deserted Lisbon, is the *Requiem* that the character I refer to as "I" was called on to perform in this book. Were someone to ask me why I wrote this story in Portuguese, I would answer simply that a story like this could only be written in Portuguese; it's as simple as that. But there is something else that needs explaining. Strictly speaking, a *Requiem* should be written in Latin, at least that's what tradition prescribes. Unfortunately, I don't think I'd be up to it in Latin. I realised though that I couldn't write a *Requiem* in my own language and that I required a different language, one that was for me a place of affection and reflection.

Besides being a "sonata", this *Requiem* is also a dream, during which my character will meet both the living and the dead on equal terms: people, things and places that were, perhaps, in need of a prayer, a prayer that my character can only express in his own way, through a novel. But this book is, above all, a homage to a country I adopted and which, in turn, adopted me, to a people who liked me as much as I liked them.

Should anyone remark that this *Requiem* was not performed with due solemnity, I cannot but agree. But the fact is that I chose to play my music not on an organ, which is an instrument proper to cathedrals, but on a mouth-organ that you can carry about in your pocket, or on a barrel-organ that you can wheel through the streets. Like Carlos Drummond de Andrade, I've always had a fondness for street music and I agree with him when he says: "I have no desire to be friends with Handel, I've never heard the dawn chorus of the archangels. I'm happy with the noises that drift up from the street, which bear no message and are lost, just as we are lost."

A.T.

THE CHARACTERS
ENCOUNTERED IN THIS BOOK

The Young Junky
The Lame Lottery-Ticket Seller
The Taxi Driver
The Waiter at the Brasileira
The Old Gypsy Woman
The Cemetery Keeper
Tadeus
Senhor Casimiro
Senhor Casimiro's Wife
The Porter at the Pensão Isadora
Isadora
Viriata
My Father as a Young Man
The Barman at the Museum of Ancient Art
The Copyist
The Ticket Collector
The Lighthousekeeper's Wife
The Manager of the Casa do Alentejo
Isabel
The Seller of Stories
Mariazinha
My Guest
The Accordionist

REQUIEM

I

I THOUGHT: the guy isn't going to turn up. And then I thought: I can't call him a "guy," he's a great poet, perhaps the greatest poet of the twentieth century, he died years ago, I should treat him with respect or, at least, with deference. Meanwhile, however, I was beginning to get fed up. The Late July sun was blazing down and I thought: Here I am on holiday, I was having a really nice time at my friends' house in the country in Azeitão, so why did I agree to this meeting here on the quayside?, it's utterly absurd. And, at my feet, I glimpsed the silhouette of my shadow and that seemed absurd to me too, incongruous, senseless; it was a brief shadow, crushed by the midday sun, and it was then that I remembered: He said twelve o'clock, but perhaps he meant twelve o'clock at night, because that's when ghosts appear, at midnight. I got up and walked along the quayside. The traffic along the avenue had almost stopped, only a few cars passed now, some with sunshades on their roofracks, people going to the beaches at Caparica, it was after all a sweltering hot day. I thought: What am I doing here in Lisbon on the last Sunday in July?, and I started walking faster in order to reach Santos as quickly as possible, it might be a little cooler in the small park there."

The park was deserted, apart from the man at the newspaper stand. I went over to him and the man smiled. Have you read the news?, he asked cheerily, Benfica won. I shook my head, no, I hadn't seen the news yet, and the man said: it was an evening game in Spain, a benefit match. I bought the sports paper, *A Bola*, and chose a bench to sit down on. I was reading about the shot that had given Benfica the winning goal against Real Madrid, when I heard someone say: Good afternoon, and I looked up. Good afternoon, repeated the unshaven youth standing in front of me, I need your help. Help? For what?, I asked. Food, he said, I haven't eaten for two days. He was a young man in his twenties, wearing jeans and a shirt, and was timidly holding out his hand to me, as if asking for alms. He was blond and had bags under his eyes. You mean you haven't had a fix for two days, I said instinctively, and the young man replied: it comes to the same thing, drugs are food too, at least for me they are. In theory, I'm in favour of all drugs, I said, soft and hard, but only in theory, in practice I'm against them, I'm afraid I'm one of those bourgeois intellectuals full of prejudices and I don't think it's right that you should take drugs in a public park, that you should make such a distressing spectacle of your body, I'm sorry, but it's against my principles, I might be able to accept you taking drugs in the privacy of your own home, as people used to do, in the company of intelligent and cultivated friends, listening to Mozart or Erik Satie. By the way, I added, do you like Erik Satie? The Young Junky looked at me in surprise. Is he a friend of yours? he asked. No, I said, he's a French composer, he was part of the avant-garde movement, a great composer from the age of surrealism, if one can speak of surrealism as belonging to an age, he wrote mostly for the piano, a deeply neurotic man I believe, like you and me perhaps, I'd like to have known him but we were born into different ages. Just two hundred *escudos*, said the Young Junky, two hundred *escudos* is all I need, I've got the rest of the money, Camarão will be along in half an hour, he's the dealer, I need another fix, I'm getting withdrawal symptoms. The Young Junky took a handkerchief out of his pocket and blew his nose loudly. He had tears in his eyes. You're not being fair, he said, I could have been aggressive, I could have threatened you, I could have played the hardened addict, but no, I was friendly, pleasant, we even chatted about music, and you still won't give me two hundred *escudos*, it's incredible. He blew his nose again and went on: Besides, the one hundred *escudo* notes are cool, they've got a picture of Fernando Pessoa on them, and now let me ask *you* a question, do you like Pessoa? Very much, I replied, I could even tell you a good story about him, but it's not worth it, I feel a bit strange, I've just come from the Cais de Alcântara, but there was no one there, and I intend going back there at midnight, do you understand? No, I don't, said the Young Junky, but it doesn't matter, and thanks. He slipped the two hundred *escudos* I was holding out to him into his pocket, then blew his nose again. Right, he said, if you'll excuse me, I have to go and look for Camarão now, I'm sorry, I really enjoyed talking to you, have a nice day, goodbye.

I leaned back on the bench and closed my eyes. It was horribly hot, I didn't feel like reading *A Bola* any more, maybe it was hunger, but I couldn't really be bothered to get up and go off in search of a restaurant, I preferred to stay there, in the shade, barely breathing.

It's the big draw tomorrow, said a voice, wouldn't you like to buy a lottery ticket? I opened my eyes. The voice belonged to a small man in his seventies, who was dressed modestly but bore on his face and in his manner the traces of a former dignity. He came limping over to me and I thought: I know this man, and then I said to him: Just a moment, we've met before somewhere, you're the Lame Lottery-Ticket Seller, I know you from somewhere else. Where?, asked the man, sitting down on my bench and breathing a sigh of relief. I don't know, I said, I couldn't say now, I just have an absurd feeling, the idea that I've come across you in a book somewhere, but it might just be the heat, or hunger, heat and hunger can play funny tricks on you sometimes. I have the feeling you've got quite a few odd ideas, said the old man, forgive me for saying so, but you do seem a touch obsessive. No, I said, that's not my problem, my problem is that I don't know why I'm here, it's as if it were all a hallucination, I can't really explain it to you, I don't even know what I mean, let's just say I was in Azeitão, do you know Azeitão?, well, that's where I was, at a friends' house, in their garden, sitting under a big tree there, a mulberry tree I think, I was stretched out in a deckchair reading a book I particularly like and then I suddenly found myself here, ah, now I remember, it was in *The Book of Disquiet*, you're the Lame Lottery-Ticket Seller who was always bothering Bernardo Soares, that's where I met you, in the book I was reading under the mulberry tree in the garden of a farmhouse in Azeitão. I know all about disquiet, said the

14

Lame Lottery-Ticket Seller, and sometimes I feel as if I'd walked out of a book too, a book full of splendid illustrations, richly laid tables, finely furnished rooms, but the rich man died, and the only Bernardo in the story was my brother, Bernardo António Pereira de Melo, he was the one who squandered the family fortune, London, Paris, prostitutes and, before I knew it, the lands we owned in the North had been sold for next to nothing, an operation in Houston for cancer saw off the rest, the money in the bank ran out and here I am, selling lottery tickets. He paused for breath and said: By the way, forgive me, I don't wish to be rude, but since I've been addressing you formally as "o senhor", right from the start, I don't quite understand why you've been addressing me as "você", allow me to introduce myself, my name's Francisco Maria Pereira de Melo, delighted to meet you. I'm sorry, I said, I'm Italian and I sometimes get confused over the different forms of address, they're so complicated in Portuguese, forgive me. We can speak in English if you prefer, said the Lame Lottery-Ticket Seller, the problem doesn't arise in English, they just use "you" all the time, and my English is good, or perhaps you'd prefer French, there's no confusion there either, it's always "vous", I speak excellent French as well. No, I replied, I'd rather speak Portuguese, this is a Portuguese adventure after all, and I don't want to step outside my adventure.

The Lame Lottery-Ticket Seller stretched out his legs and leaned back on the bench. And now, if you'll forgive me, he said, I'm going to read for a bit, I devote a few hours every day to reading. He took a book out of his pocket. It was a magazine, *Esprit*, and he said: I'm reading

an article about the soul by a French philosopher, it's
odd to read things about the soul again, for a long time
it's hardly been spoken of at all, at least not since the
1940s, now it seems that the soul is back in fashion,
people are rediscovering it, I'm not a Catholic but I
believe in the soul in the vital, collective sense, perhaps
even in a Spinozist sense, do you believe in the soul? It's
one of the few things I do believe in, I said, at least at
this moment, in this garden where we're sitting and talking, it's my soul that was the cause of all this, I mean,
I'm not sure if it's my soul exactly, perhaps it's my
Unconscious, because it was my Unconscious that
brought me here. Hold on, said the Lame Lottery-Ticket
Seller, the Unconscious, what does that mean?, the
Unconscious is something found in the Viennese bour-
geoisie at the turn of the century, we're in Portugal here
and you yourself are Italian, we belong to the South, to
the Graeco-Roman civilisation, we have nothing to do
with Central Europe, no, *we* have soul. That's true, I
said, I do have a soul, you're right, but I have an Unconscious too, I mean, *now* I do, you see, the Unconscious
is something you catch, it's like a disease, I just happened
to catch the virus of the Unconscious.

The Lame Lottery-Ticket Seller regarded me with an
air of despondency. Look, he said, do you want to do a
swap? I'll lend you my *Esprit* and you lend me *A Bola*.
But I thought you were interested in the soul, I objected.
I was, he said resignedly, but my subscription runs out
after this issue and I'm beginning to grow into my role
now, I'm turning into the Lame Lottery-Ticket Seller,
I'm more interested in the goal Benfica scored. All right,
I said, in that case, I'd like to buy a lottery ticket, have

you got a number that ends in a nine?, you see, nine is my month, I was born in September, and I'd like to buy a lottery ticket that includes that number. I do indeed, sir, said the Lame Lottery-Ticket Seller, when were you born exactly?, because I was born in September too. I was born at the time of the Autumn Equinox, I said, when the moon is mad and the ocean swells. A most fortunate moment to be born, said the Lame Lottery-Ticket Seller, you're in for some good luck. I certainly need it, I replied, paying him for the ticket, but not on the lottery, I need it for today, today is a very strange day for me, I'm dreaming but what I dream seems to me to be real, and I have to meet certain people who exist only in my memory. Today is the last Sunday in July, said the Lame Lottery-Ticket Seller, the city is deserted, it must be forty degrees in the shade, I should think it's the best day there is for meeting people who only exist in memories, your soul, I mean, your Unconscious is going to be kept very busy on a day like today, I wish you a good afternoon and good luck.

II

I'M TERRIBLY SORRY, said the Taxi Driver, but I don't know where Rua das Pedras Negras is, could you give me some directions? He smiled a smile full of white teeth and went on: I'm from São Tomé, you see, I've only been working in Lisbon for a month and I don't know the streets yet, in my own country I was an engineer but nothing needs engineering there, so here I am working as a taxi driver and I don't even know the streets, I mean I know the city really well, I never get lost, it's just that I don't know the *names* of the streets. Oh, I said, it's a street I know from twenty-five years back and *I* can't remember how to get there either, though I know it's near the castle. Let's head in that direction then, said the Taxi Driver, smiling, and we set off.

Only then did I realise that I was sweating profusely. My shirt was drenched and it clung to my chest and back. I took off my jacket, but even then I went on sweating. Look, I said, perhaps you can help me, my shirt's sopping wet, I need to buy a new one, can you suggest where I might go? The Taxi Driver braked and turned to me. Do you feel ill?, he asked, a worried expression on his face. No, I replied, I don't know, I mean I don't think so, it must be the heat, the heat and some sort of anxiety attack, sometimes anxiety can make you sweat, anyway I need a clean shirt to put on. The man lit a cigarette and thought for a moment. Today's Sunday, he said, the shops are all shut. I tried to wind down the window on my side, but the handle was broken. This fact only increased my anxiety, I could feel the sweat pouring from my head and a few drops fell onto my knees. The Taxi Driver was looking at me with real concern now. Then he said, I know, I've got a great idea, I'll give you my shirt, if you don't mind wearing it that is. You can't do that, I said, you can't drive around naked from the waist up. I've got a T-shirt on underneath, he replied, I can just wear that. But there must be somewhere in the whole of Lisbon where I can buy a shirt, I said, perhaps a shopping centre, a market, I don't know. Carcavelos! exclaimed the Taxi Driver triumphantly, there must be a Sunday market in Carcavelos, that's where I live, my wife goes shopping there every Sunday, or is it Thursday? I don't know, I said, I'm not sure that's a very good idea, there's a beach at Carcavelos and today's Sunday, it'll be packed, it could be dreadful, can't you think of anywhere here in Lisbon? The man struck his forehead with the palm of his hand. The gypsies! he exclaimed, I'd forgotten about the gypsies! He smiled his broad, candid smile again and said: Don't you worry, my friend, you'll get your shirt, I've just remembered that on Sundays the gypsies set up stalls at the entrance to the Cemitério dos Prazeres, they sell everything, shoes, socks, shirts, T-shirts, let's try them, the only problem is I don't know how to get there, I mean, I know vaguely where the Cemitério dos Prazeres is, but I don't know which route to take, can you help me at all? Let's see, I said, I'm a bit confused too, let's review the situation, where are we now? We're at Cais do Sodré, said the Taxi Driver, on the avenue, almost opposite the station. Right, I said, I think I know how to get there, but to start with let's go up Rua do Alecrim, I'd like to drop in at the Brasileira to buy a bottle of wine. The Taxi Driver drove round the square and set off up Rua do Alecrim, he switched on the radio and gave me a sideways look. Are you sure you're OK?, he asked. I reassured him and leaned back in the seat. Now I really was bathed in sweat. I undid the top buttons of my shirt and rolled up the sleeves. I'll wait here with the engine running, said the man, stopping on the corner of Largo Camões, but do be quick, because if a policeman turns up, he'll move me on. I got out of the taxi. The Chiado was deserted apart from a woman, dressed in black and carrying a plastic bag, who was sitting at the foot of the statue of António Ribeiro Chiado. I went into the Brasileira and the barman gave me a mocking look, did you fall in the river?, he asked. Worse than that, I said, I seem to have a river inside me, do you have any French champagne? Laurent-Perrier and Veuve Clicquot, he said, they're both the same price and they're nice and chilled. Which would you recommend? I asked. Look, he said, with the air of one who knows about such things, they're always advertising Veuve Clicquot, to read the magazines you'd think it was the best champagne in the world, but I find it a touch acidic, besides I don't like widows, I never have, anyway, if I were you, I'd buy the Laurent-Perrier, especially since, as I said, it's exactly the same price. Fine, I said, I'll take the Laurent-Perrier. The barman opened the fridge, wrapped the bottle up and put it in a plastic bag on which was written in red letters: "A Brasileira do Chiado, the oldest café in Lisbon". I paid, went out into the sun again, still sweating like mad, and got into the taxi. Right, said the Taxi Driver, now you have to tell me the way. It's easy, I said, drive into Largo Camões and where Silva's the jeweller's is, take the road going down, it's called Calçada do Combro, then take Calçada da Estrela and when you reach Largo da Estrela, go up Domingos Sequeiros as far as Campo de Ourique, and then on the left you'll find Saraiva de Carvalho which will take us straight to Largo do Cemitério dos Prazeres. You'll have to tell me the streets one at a time, my friend, said the Taxi Driver pulling out, I'm sorry but you'll have to be patient. I said, let me just close my eyes for a minute or two, I'm exhausted, look, it's easy to remember: Calçada do Combro, Calçada da Estrela, Largo da Estrela, Domingos Sequeiros, Campo de Ourique, and when we get there I'll tell you.

I'd finally managed to open the window, but the air that entered was hot. I closed my eyes and thought about other things, about my childhood, I remembered how in summer I used to go on my bike to fetch cold water from the "Le Caroline" with a bottle and a straw basket. The car braked suddenly and I opened my eyes. The driver had got out of the taxi and was looking about him disconsolately. I've taken the wrong road, he said, look, I've come up the wrong road, we're in Campo de Ourique, I took the road on the left as you said, but I don't think it was Saraiva de Carvalho, I took another road and it's one-way only, see what I mean?, all the cars are parked facing in the other direction, I've come up a one-way street. It doesn't matter, I said, the important thing is that you turned left, now we can just drive along this one-way street until we reach Largo dos Prazeres. The Taxi Driver placed his hand on his heart and said very gravely: I can't, I'm sorry but I really can't, I still haven't sorted out my taxi licence and if a policeman sees me, he'll slap a huge fine on me and then what will become of me? I'll have to go back to São Tomé, that's what, I'm sorry, but I really can't do it. Look, I said, the city's empty today, anyway, don't worry, if a policeman stops us, I'll talk to him, I'll pay the fine, I'll take full responsibility, I promise, please, I'm sweating like a pig here, I need a shirt, or even two shirts, please, you don't want me to get ill here in this unknown street in Campo de Ourique, do you?

I didn't mean to threaten him, I was being serious, but he clearly took my words as a threat, because he scrambled back into the taxi and drove off without a word of protest. If that's what you want, he said, in a resigned voice, I don't want you being ill in my taxi, I haven't got my licence yet, you see, it would ruin me. We drove the wrong way down the length of the street which, for all I know, may well have been Saraiva de Carvalho itself, and came out in Largo dos Prazeres. The gypsies were right by the entrance to the cemetery, they'd set out a small market on wooden tables and blankets spread on the ground. I got out of the taxi and asked the driver to wait for me. The Largo was empty and the gypsies were stretched out asleep on the pavement. I went over to a table occupied by an old gypsy woman dressed all in black but for the yellow scarf on her head. On her table lay a pile of Lacoste polo shirts, perfect but for the absence of the crocodile. Excuse me, I said, I'd like to buy something. What's wrong with you, my dear?, asked the Old Gypsy Woman when she saw my shirt, have you got the fever or something? I don't know what's wrong with me, I replied, I've been sweating like mad and I need a clean shirt, possibly two. I'll tell you what's wrong with you in a minute, said the Old Gypsy Woman, but first, my dear, buy the shirts, you can't go around like that, if you leave sweat to dry on your back it can make you ill. What do you think would be best, I asked, a shirt or a polo shirt? The Old Gypsy Woman appeared to think for a moment. Then she said, I'd advise you to buy a Lacoste polo shirt, they're nice and cool, it's five hundred *escudos* for a fake Lacoste and five hundred and twenty for a genuine one. My God, I said, a Lacoste shirt for five hundred and twenty *escudos* seems very cheap, but what's the difference between a fake one and a genuine one? That's easy, said the Old Gypsy Woman, if you want a genuine Lacoste shirt, you buy a fake one, which costs five hundred *escudos*, and then you buy a crocodile, which costs twenty *escudos* and is self-adhesive, you stick the crocodile on in the right place and there's your genuine Lacoste shirt. She showed me a small bag full of crocodiles. What's more, she said, for twenty *escudos*, my dear, I'll give you four crocodiles, so that you'll have three spare, because the trouble with these self-adhesive things is that they're always coming unstuck. That seems very reasonable to me, I said, I'll buy two genuine Lacostes then, which colour would you recommend? I like red and black best myself, she said, because they're the gypsy colours, but black's no good in this sun, besides you're obviously rather delicate, and red's too loud, you're too old now for this colour red. I'm not that old, I protested, I can still wear bright colours. I'd go for the blue, said the Old Gypsy Woman, I think blue would be ideal for you and now, my dear, I'm going to tell you what's wrong with you and why you're sweating so much, look, for another two hundred *escudos*, I'll tell you everything, what's happening to you now and what else awaits you on this hot Sunday afternoon, wouldn't you like to know your fate? The Old Gypsy Woman grabbed my left hand and looked hard at my palm. It's rather complicated, my dear, said the Old Gypsy Woman, you'd best sit down here on this bench. I sat down, but she didn't let go of my hand. Listen, my dear, she said, this can't go on, you can't live in two worlds at once, in the world of reality and the world of dreams, that kind of thing leads to hallucinations, you're like a sleepwalker walking through a landscape with your arms outstretched, and everything you touch becomes part of your dream, even me, a fat old woman weighing one hundred seventy-five, I can feel myself dissolving into the air at the touch of your hand, as if I was becoming part of your dream too. What should I do?, I asked, tell me. Right now, you can't do anything, she replied, the day still awaits you and you can't run away from it, you can't escape your fate, it will be a day of tribulations but also a day of purification, afterwards, my dear, you may perhaps be able to feel at peace with yourself, at least I hope so. The Old Gypsy Woman lit a cigar and inhaled the smoke. Now give me your right hand, she said, so that I can finish my reading. She looked closely at my right hand and stroked the palm with her rough fingers. I see that you have to visit someone, she said, but the house you're looking for exists only in your memory or in your dream, you can tell the taxi not to wait for you, the person you're looking for is right here, on the other side of that gate. She pointed in the direction of the cemetery and said, off you go, my love, you have an appointment to keep. I thanked her and went over to the Taxi Driver. It looks like I'm going to stay here, I said, getting out my wallet to pay him, anyway, thanks very much, you've been really kind. Great polo shirts, said the Taxi Driver, looking at the two folded shirts under my arm, you made a good choice there. I paid him and picked up my jacket and the bottle of champagne. The Taxi Driver shook me energetically by the hand and gave me a card. My phone number, he said, if you ever need a taxi again, just phone, my wife will take the message, you can even book a taxi for the next day, if you want. The car drove off, but after only a few yards, reversed back towards me. You're not still feeling ill, are you?, the man asked from his window. No, I said, I'm better now, thanks. The Taxi Driver smiled and the car disappeared round the corner.

I went through the gate into the cemetery. There was no one there, just a cat strolling amongst the graves nearest the gate. To my right, at the entrance itself, right next to the gate, was a small lodge, the door was open. Excuse me, I said, can I come in? I closed my eyes to accustom them to the darkness, because the room lay in deep shadow. I managed to make out a few coffins piled one on top of the other, a vase of dried flowers and a table with a gravestone leaning against it. Come in, said a voice, and I saw that at the far end of the room, near a vast sideboard, sat a small man. He was wearing glasses and a grey overall and, on his head, a black cap with a plastic peak, like the ones worn by ticket collectors on trains. What can I do for you, sir?, he asked, the cemetery's closed, it'll be open again soon, it's lunch time now, I'm the cemetery keeper. Only then did I realise he was having his lunch. He was eating out of a small aluminium tin and was poised with his spoon in mid-air. I'm sorry, I said, I didn't mean to disturb you, do forgive me. Would you care to join me?, asked the Cemetery Keeper, carrying on eating. No, thank you, I said, enjoy your meal but, if you don't mind, I'll just wait here until you've finished, or I could wait outside if you'd rather. *Feijoada*, said the Cemetery Keeper as if he hadn't heard me, every day it's *feijoada*, my wife doesn't know how to cook anything else. And then he went on: Certainly not, you wait here in the cool, you can't wait out there in that heat, sit down, find somewhere to sit and sit down. That's very kind of you, I said, would you mind if I changed my shirt too? I was drenched in sweat and so I bought two polo shirts from the gypsies. I placed the bottle of champagne on a coffin, took off my shirt and put on the "genuine Lacoste". I was feeling better, I'd stopped sweating and the room was really cool. I first came here as a boy, said the Cemetery Keeper, fifty years ago now, and I've spent my life keeping watch over the dead. Really, I said. A silence fell between us. The man went on calmly eating his *feijoada*, from time to time taking off his glasses and putting them back on again. I can't see a thing without my glasses, he said, or with them for that matter, everything's blurred, the doctor says it's a cataplasm. A cataract, I said, the word's "cataract". Well, cataract or cataplasm, it makes no difference, said the Cemetery Keeper, it comes to the same rotten thing. He took off his cap and scratched his head. What's the idea of coming to the cemetery at this hour and in this heat?, asked the Keeper, you must be mad. A friend of mine is here, I replied, the gypsy told me so, the gypsy selling polo shirts outside said I should look for him in here, he's an old friend, we spent a lot of time together, we were like brothers, I'd like to pay him a visit, there's a question I'd like to ask him. And do you think he'll reply?, said the Cemetery Keeper, the dead tend to be very silent, I should know, I know them. I'm going to try, I said, there's something I've never understood, he died without explaining it to me. Something to do with women?, asked the Cemetery Keeper. I didn't reply and he went on: There's always a woman somewhere in these stories. It wasn't only that, I said, there may have been some malice involved, I don't know how to explain, but I'd like to understand the reason for that malice, if that's what it was. What was his name?, asked the Cemetery Keeper. Tadeus, I said, Tadeus Waclaw. That's some name, said the Keeper. He was the son of Polish parents, I explained, but he wasn't Polish himself, he was well and truly Portuguese, he even chose a Portuguese pseudonym. And what did he do?, asked the Keeper. Well, I said, he worked, but he was mainly a writer, he wrote some lovely things in Portuguese, well, lovely isn't quite the word, the things he wrote were bitter, because he himself was full of pain and bitterness. The Cemetery Keeper pushed aside his lunch tin and got up, he went over to the vast sideboard and picked up a large book, like the registers teachers use in school. What's his surname?, he asked. Slowacki, I said, Tadeus Waclaw Slowacki. Is he buried under his real name or under his pseudonym?, asked the Keeper, quite rightly in the circumstances. I don't know, I replied, perplexed, but I think he was buried under his real name, that seems more logical to me. Silva, Silva, Silva, Silva, Silva, Silva . . . Slowacki, said the Keeper at last, here he is, Slowacki Tadeus Waclaw, first row on the right, no. 4664. The Keeper took off his glasses and smiled. It's a reversible number, he said, did your friend like to joke? He did, I said, he spent his whole life playing jokes, he even played jokes on himself. I'm going to write that number down, said the Keeper, I like reversible numbers, I'm going to try it on the lottery, sometimes it's odd finds like this that turn out to be really lucky.

I thanked him and said goodbye. I picked up my bottle of champagne and went out into the heat. I found the first row on the right and began walking slowly along it. I was feeling terribly anxious again and my heart was pounding hard. It was a modest grave, just a headstone placed on the ground. There he was with his Polish name and above his name was a photograph that I recognised. It was a full-length photograph, he was wearing a shirt with the sleeves rolled up and was leaning against a boat, behind him you could see the sea. I had taken that photograph in 1965, it was in Caparica in September and we were so happy, he'd just got out of prison a week before, thanks to the pressure of public opinion abroad, a French newspaper had said: "The Salazar régime must free all writers," and there he was, leaning against the boat with the French newspaper in his hands. I went closer to see if I could read the name of the paper, but I couldn't, it was out of focus in the photograph, other times, I thought, time swallowed up everything, and then I said:

Hello, Tadeus, it's me, I've come to visit you. And then I said it again, more loudly this time: Hello Tadeus, it's me, I've come to visit you.

III

COME ON IN THEN, said Tadeus' voice, you know the
way. I closed the door behind me and walked along the
corridor. It was dark and I stumbled into a pile of things
that toppled over. I paused to pick up the objects I'd
stumbled into: books, a wooden toy, the sort you buy at
fairs, a Barcelos cockerel, a small statue of a saint, the
figure of a friar bought in Caldas* with a huge penis
protruding from beneath his habit. Bumping into things
always was your speciality, I heard Tadeus' voice say from
the next room. And yours was collecting junk, I replied,
you're stony broke and you go and buy a friar with his
willy hanging out, when will you grow up, Tadeus? I
heard a guffaw, then Tadeus appeared at the door, sil-
houetted against the light. Come in, he said, come in,
don't be shy, this is the house I've always lived in, the
house where you ate, slept, fucked, don't tell me you
don't recognise it? It isn't that, I protested, it's just that
there are a few matters I need to clear up, you died
without telling me anything, and I've spent years agonis-
ing over it, now it's time that I knew, I'm free now,

* Barcelos and Caldas are two towns in north and central Portugal respectively,
both famous for their ceramics.

today I feel extraordinarily free, look, I've even lost my
Super-Ego, it just reached its expiry date, like milk in a
carton, I mean it, I feel free, liberated, that's why I'm
here. Have you had lunch?, asked Tadeus. No, I said, I
had breakfast in the garden where I was this morning,
but I haven't eaten anything since. Let's go and get something to eat then, said Tadeus, down the road, in
Casimiro's place, just wait till you see what's in store for
you, yesterday I ordered a *sarrabulho à moda do Douro*,
which was out of this world, Casimiro's wife is actually
from the Douro and she makes a divine *sarrabulho*, you
could die a happy man once you've eaten it, do you know
what I mean? I don't know what a *sarrabulho* is, I said,
doubtless something lethal, like all your favourite dishes,
I bet it's got pork in it, you always adored pork, you're
even prepared to eat it on a blazing hot day like today,
but before we go to the restaurant I have to talk to you,
I even brought a bottle of champagne, it's probably warm
by now, but we could put some ice cubes in the glasses,
here it is, it's a Laurent-Perrier, I bought it in the Café
Brasileira in the Chiado. Tadeus took charge of the bottle
and went off to look for some glasses. Let's talk in the
restaurant, if you don't mind that is, he said from the
kitchen, be patient, it would be best to talk about
the things *you* want to talk about in the restaurant, here
we can drink the champagne and talk about literature.
He returned with the glasses and the ice. Let's sit down,
he said, let's drink our champagne sitting down. He
stretched out on the sofa and waved me into the armchair
by his side. It's just like old times, he said, but don't
lecture me about food and pork, I'm going to die in a
few years' time of a coronary and here you are giving me

lectures, forget it, don't go on at me. All right, I said, I didn't mean to go on at you, but I think you owe me an explanation. All in good time, said Tadeus, with a dish of *sarrabulho* in front of us, wouldn't you rather talk about literature now, so much more refined? OK, I replied, let's talk about literature, what are you writing at the moment? A short novel in verse, he said, a story about a love affair between a bishop and a nun, it takes place in seventeenth-century Portugal, it's a rather sombre story, possibly obscene, a metaphor for debasement, what do you think of the idea? I don't know, I said, do they eat *sarrabulho* in your story? From what you've said it sounds like the sort of story that needs *sarrabulho*. Anyway, here's health, said Tadeus, raising his glass, you're the one with the soul, my fearful friend, I only have a body, and I haven't even got that for much longer. I haven't got a soul any more, I replied, now I have an Unconscious, it's a virus I caught, and that's why I'm here in your house, that's how come I found you. Well, here's to your Unconscious then, said Tadeus, filling the glasses again, another couple of drinks and then off to Casimiro's. We drank in silence. From the barracks on the other side of the road came the sound of a trumpet. Somewhere a clock chimed the hours. We'd better go, said Tadeus, if we don't, Casimiro's will be closed. I got up and walked back down the corridor on unsteady legs, feeling the effect of the champagne. We left his house and walked down the street. The small square was full of pigeons. A soldier was stretched out on a bench by the fountain. We walked along arm in arm, keeping step with each other. Tadeus seemed more serious now, less jokey, as if troubled by something. What's wrong,

Tadeus?, I asked. I don't know, he said, maybe it's just an attack of melancholy, I miss the days when we used to stroll round the city like this, do you remember?, everything was different then, everything seemed brighter, cleaner somehow. Youth, I said, our eyes saw things differently then. I'm really glad you came to see me though, he said, it's the best present you could give me, we couldn't just say goodbye the way we did, you're right, we really do need to talk about that whole sad business. I stopped and made Tadeus stop too. Look, Tadeus, I said, the really mysterious thing, the thing that most intrigues me is the note you'll give me the day you die, do you remember? You're at death's door, lying on your bed of pain in Santa Maria hospital, there's a monstrous machine by your side to which you're attached, you've got a tube up your nose and a drip in your right arm, you gesture to me to move closer, I do, you indicate with your left hand that you want to write something, I find a piece of paper and a pen and I give them to you, your eyes look dull and you have death written on your face, you make an enormous effort to write, using your left hand, and then you give me the note and on it is this really odd sentence, Tadeus, what did you mean by it? I don't know, he said, I can't remember, I was dying, how do you expect me to remember? Besides, he went on, I don't even know what the sentence was, why don't you tell me? All right, I said, the sentence went like this: *Blame it all on herpes zoster*, honestly, Tadeus, is that any kind of sentence to say goodbye with, to leave with a friend when you're dying? Listen, my fearful friend, he said, there are two possibilities: either I was completely out of it and I was writing things that have no meaning, or I was just playing a trick on you, I spent my whole life playing tricks on people, you know that, I played them on you, on everyone, it was my last prank, and thus dies Tadeus, with a final pirouette, *olé*! I don't know why, Tadeus, I said, but I always connected that idiotic phrase with Isabel, that's really why I'm here, it's her I want to talk about. Later, he said, walking on.

We had reached the restaurant. Senhor Casimiro was leaning in the doorway, a white apron covering his enormous belly. Good afternoon, Senhor Casimiro, Tadeus said in greeting, I've got a surprise for you, do you recognise this man?, you don't remember him, eh? Well he's an old friend come back from the void on this blazing hot day, he's come to see me again before I go to the devil once and for all, and I've invited him to eat *sarrabulho*. Senhor Casimiro solicitously opened the door for us and let us pass. An excellent idea, excellent, he exclaimed, waddling after us into the large empty room, where would you like to sit?, today you have the whole restaurant at your disposal. Tadeus chose a table in a corner, beneath the fan. Senhor Casimiro's restaurant was lovely. The floor was laid with black and white slabs of marble, the walls lined with blue and white tiles from the early part of the century. In the opposite corner of the room, near the kitchen, was a parrot on a perch, who every now and then let out a cry: Just as well! Senhor Casimiro arrived bearing bread, butter and olives. With *sarrabulho* you really ought to drink red wine, he said, but I don't know if your friend would like that, I have a Reguengos in the cellar that I can heartily recommend. The

Reguengos is fine by me, said Tadeus. I nodded and sighed: All right, but it'll finish me off.

The *sarrabulho* was served in an earthenware dish, the traditional type, terracotta with yellow flowers painted on it in relief. At first glance, it looked revolting. In the middle of the dish were the potatoes, roasted in fat, surrounded by chunks of pork and tripe. The whole thing was drenched in a brown sauce that was probably made from wine or cooked blood, I hadn't the slightest idea which. It's the first time I've ever eaten anything like this, I said, I've been coming to Portugal for years and years, I've travelled the country from north to south and I've never felt brave enough to eat this, today will be the death of me, I'll get food poisoning. You won't regret it, Tadeus said, serving me, eat up, my fearful friend, and stop talking nonsense. I stuck a fork into a bit of pork, almost closing my eyes to do so, and raised it to my lips. It was delicious, it had the subtlest of flavours. Tadeus saw this and looked delighted, his eyes shining. It's wonderful, I said, you're right, it's one of the most delicious things I've eaten in my whole life. Just as well! croaked the parrot. I second the parrot, said Tadeus, and poured me a glass of Reguengos. We ate in silence. Now, my fearful friend, said Tadeus, why have you come? I've already told you, I replied, because of that note you'll write to me before you die, because I'm obsessed by those words, Tadeus, and I want to live in peace, I want you to rest in peace too, I want peace for all of us, Tadeus, that's why I'm here, but I'm here too because of another idea that obsesses me, because of Isabel, but I'll tell you about that later. All right, said Tadeus, and he made a sign to Senhor Casimiro. Senhor Casimiro must call his wife, said Tadeus, we must offer her our congratulations. Senhor Casimiro disappeared into the kitchen and shortly afterwards a woman in a white overall came out. She was plump and had a faint moustache. Did you enjoy it?, she asked, looking embarrassed. We adored it, said Tadeus, my friend says it's the best thing he's eaten in his entire life. He looked at me and said: Tell her, my friend. I told Senhor Casimiro's Wife and she looked even more embarrassed. They're just simple dishes, she said, things people in my village used to cook, it was my mother who taught me. Simple my eye, replied Tadeus, don't talk nonsense, Casimira, there's nothing simple about this, it's a work of art. Senhor Tadeus will have his little joke, said Senhor Casimiro's Wife, and I've already told you not to call me Casimira, my name's Maria da Conceição. But Casimiro's wife should be called Casimira, said Tadeus, I'm sorry Casimira, but that's decided, and now explain to this young man how you make *sarrabulho à moda do Douro*, so that he can return to his own country and make it at home, because where he lives they only ever eat spaghetti. Really?, asked Senhor Casimiro's Wife. Absolutely, said Tadeus, they eat nothing but spaghetti. No, no, said Senhor Casimiro's Wife, even more embarrassed, I didn't mean that, I meant does your friend really want to know how to make *sarrabulho*. Of course I do, I said, I'd love to know the recipe, if you don't mind telling me that is. First, you'll have to forgive me, sir, said Senhor Casimiro's Wife, because where I come from, the real *sarrabulho* is served with *polenta*, but I didn't have any maize flour today so I used potatoes, but anyway I'll tell you the ingredients for a real *sarrabulho*, I never measure anything, I do everything by eye, anyway, you need loin of pork, fat, lard, pig's liver, tripe, a bowl of cooked blood, a whole bulb of garlic, a glass of white wine, an onion, oil, salt, pepper and cumin. Sit down, Casimira, said Tadeus, and have a little glass of this Reguengos de Monsaraz, it'll help you to explain even better. Senhor Casimiro's Wife thanked Tadeus, sat down and accepted the glass of wine he offered her. Right, said Senhor Casimiro's Wife, if you want to make a good *sarrabulho* you have to prepare the meat the night before, cut the pork into cubes and marinate it with the chopped garlic, wine, salt, pepper and cumin, by the next day the meat will be really tender and will smell delicious, next you take an earthenware dish and add the chopped up fat from the *folhos*, that's what the fat joining the intestines together is called, and let it melt over a low flame, brown the cubed pork in the lard over a high flame and then leave to cook slowly. When the meat is almost done, pour over the marinade from the night before and let it boil off. Meanwhile, cut up the tripe and the liver and fry it all in the lard until it's nicely browned. Then fry the chopped onion in the oil and add it to the bowl of cooked blood. Then mix everything together in the earthenware dish and the *sarra-bulho* is ready, flavour with more cumin if you want and serve with potatoes, *polenta* or rice, as I said I prefer *polenta* because that's how they serve it where I come from, but that's entirely up to you.

Senhor Casimiro's Wife gave an exhausted sigh and placed a hand on her heaving bosom. And there you are, she said, after that your stomach does all the work, you just have to eat it up. Bravo! exclaimed Tadeus, applauding, do you know what that's called, Casimira?, it's called

a first-class lesson in material culture, I've always preferred the material to the imaginary, or rather, I've always
preferred to inflame the imagination with the material,
the imagination should be handled with care, even the
collective imagination, someone should have told Herr
Jung that food always comes before the imagination. I
don't understand a word you're saying, said Senhor Casimiro's confused Wife, I haven't studied like you have, I
was brought up in a village and never got beyond primary
school. It's very simple, Casimira, said Tadeus, all I mean
is that I'm a materialist, but entirely non-dialectic, which
is what distinguishes me from the Marxists, the fact that
I'm not a dialectical materialist. You're certainly "dialectical", replied Senhor Casimiro's Wife shyly, you always
have been, ever since I've known you. That's a good one,
laughed Tadeus, slapping his knee with the palm of his
hand, Casimira deserves another glass of Reguengos for
that! No, said Senhor Casimiro's Wife, you don't want
to get me drunk, do you? That's precisely what you
should do, said Tadeus, I bet you've never been drunk
in your life, have you? You ought to drink half a bottle
of Reguengos before going to bed with Senhor Casimiro,
you'd be in seventh heaven, you and your husband.
Senhor Casimiro's Wife lowered her eyes and blushed.
Look, Senhor Tadeus, she said, it doesn't matter to me
if you choose to make fun of me, you're an educated man
and I'm just an ignorant woman, but making indecent
remarks is another matter altogether, if you don't treat me
with more respect I'll tell my husband. Senhor Casimiro
doesn't mind, replied Tadeus, he's just a dirty old man,
come on now, don't be angry, Casimira, have another
little drink and then bring us the dessert or whatever

you've prepared today, we have absolute confidence in your desserts.

Tadeus lit a cigar and offered me one. No thanks, I said, it's too strong for me. Come on, my fearful friend, he said, try it, you need a cigar after *sarrabulho*. We smoked in silence. The parrot seemed to have gone to sleep on its perch, all you could hear was the buzz of the fan. Look Tadeus, I said, why did Isabel kill herself? That's what I want to know. Tadeus inhaled the smoke and blew it out into the air again. Why don't you ask her?, he said, since you're asking me you might just as well ask her. I don't know if I'll be able to find her on this Sunday in July, I said, I found you because a gypsy woman helped me, but how can I find Isabel again? I can help you, said Tadeus, it might be easier than you think. Just tell me, I said, were you the one who persuaded her to have an abortion?

Senhor Casimiro arrived with the dessert. It was a plate of yellow cakes in the form of little boats. They're *papos de anjos de Mirandela*, said Senhor Casimiro proudly, egg yolks and fruit syrup, it's all authentic, I don't like to boast but there isn't a restaurant in Lisbon where you can eat *papos de anjos* like these. Senhor Casimiro scuttled back to the kitchen and Tadeus picked up one of the cakes. What did you want, my friend?, he said in reply to my previous question, did you want a little bastard child with two fathers? I didn't know about your affair with Isabel, I said, I only found out about it much later, you deceived me, Tadeus. And then I asked: Was it yours or mine? I don't know, he said, whoever's it was, it wouldn't have been happy. That's what you think, I replied, but I think it had the right to live. Oh yes, said Tadeus, and make four people unhappy: me, you, him and Isabel. She wasn't happy anyway, I insisted, it was because of all that that she got depressed, and it was because of the depression that she committed suicide, and that's what I want to know, if her wise counsellor was you. I've already told you, she's the one you should ask, Tadeus said defensively, I don't know, I swear, I don't know anything. You *were* the wise counsellor, I said, I see that now. That has nothing to do with her death, said Tadeus, if you want to know why she killed herself, you have to ask her. Where can I find her?, I asked. I don't know, he said, you choose a place, here or there, it makes no difference to her. In the Casa do Alentejo, I said, on Rua das Portas do Santo Antão, what do you think? Splendid, he said ironically, I'm sure it's a place she would love to have visited, I doubt she's ever set foot there before, but why not? Right, I said, at nine o'clock tonight, you can tell her I'll be waiting for her at nine o'clock tonight at the Casa do Alentejo. Let's have some coffee, said Tadeus, what I need is a coffee and a *grappa*. But Senhor Casimiro was already on his way with two coffees and a bottle of *grappa*, an old earthenware bottle. Senhor Casimiro, said Tadeus, put it all on my bill. Oh, no you don't, I cried, lunch is on me. Senhor Casimiro pretended he hadn't heard me and walked off. Don't make a fuss, said Tadeus paternally, you haven't got much money on you, you left Azeitão with hardly anything, you were sitting under a mulberry tree reading and you didn't have much money in your wallet, I know all about it, you've got the whole day ahead of you in Lisbon and you need to hang on to your cash, look, don't make a fuss. We got up and went over to the door. Senhor Casimiro and his wife leaned over the low kitchen door to say goodbye. Listen, Tadeus, I said, I need to lie down for an hour or two, I'm taking some pills that make me drowsy and this lunch you bought me is making me feel even drowsier, if I don't sleep for an hour I'll flake out on the floor. What are you taking?, he asked. It's a French drug made from amineptine, I said, it calms you down in the morning and gives you a feeling of well-being, but later on it makes you sluggish. All those drugs for the soul are junk, said Tadeus, you heal the soul through the stomach. Maybe, I said, you're lucky to be so certain about things, I'm not certain about anything. Why don't you sleep at my house?, asked Tadeus, there's a comfortable bed for you in the guestroom. Thanks, but I'd rather not, I replied, this is the last time I'll see you, but look, I really don't have much money, I can't afford a hotel, I need a cheap boarding house, one of those places where you can rent a room for an hour or two, you must know of somewhere, perhaps you can help. That's easy, he said, go to the Pensão Isadora, it's immediately behind Praça da Ribeira, mention my name and ask for Isadora, she'll give you a room, you can catch the tram that goes to Cais do Sodré, it should be here any minute.

The tram stop was right opposite the restaurant and we waited behind the glass door out of the heat. We heard the tram coming as it rounded the bend, the noise of its wheels reaching us in the silence of the city. Now are you sure you don't want to sleep at my house?, Tadeus asked again. I'm sure, I replied, goodbye Tadeus, rest in peace, I doubt we'll ever see each other again. Just as well!, cried the parrot. I opened the door, crossed the road and boarded the tram.

IV

IT WAS AN OLD BUILDING, faded pink, with rickety
wooden shutters. The guesthouse stood between a junk
shop and a shipping company and on the glass door,
which stood ajar, was written: Pensão Isadora. I pushed
open the door and went in. Behind the counter, sitting
in a wicker armchair, was a man, apparently asleep. He
had the *Correio da Manhã* draped over his face and was
snoring. I went over to him and coughed discreetly, but
the man didn't move. Then I said: Good afternoon, and
the man very slowly removed the newspaper from his face
and looked at me. He was about sixty-five years old,
possibly more, with a gaunt face and a thin moustache.
Are you the owner?, I asked. The owner isn't here, he
said in an Alentejo accent, he died a year ago, I'm the
porter. I reached for my wallet, took out my identity
card, placed it on the counter and asked: Do you need
any identification? The Porter of the Pensão Isadora gave
my identity card a questioning glance and then looked
at me distrustfully. Identification?, he said, what for? I
don't know, I said, I thought it was the custom. Look,
my friend, he said, are you trying to irritate me? I don't
want to irritate anyone, I replied patiently, I'm just
showing you my identity card. The Porter of the Pensão

Isadora got up from his chair and calmly, very calmly, picked up the card. Let's see, he murmured, you're Italian, five foot eight inches tall, you've got blue eyes and brown hair, fascinating. He dropped my identity card on the counter and said: Delighted to have met you but, if you'll excuse me, I've got to go to the lavatory, unfortunately I have problems with my prostate. He disappeared behind the grimy curtain and left me standing there; I put away my identity card and strolled round the small hallway, looking at the pictures hanging on the walls. The first was a photographic view of the Basilica in Fátima taken from a helicopter, a photograph from the fifties, perhaps, you could see the great square and an enormous queue of people going into the church. Underneath was written: *Faith knows no frontiers*. The second picture was a photograph of a simple farmhouse, also dating from the fifties to judge by the colours, and beneath that was written: *The birthplace of His Excellency the President*. The third picture was of a naked woman with blonde hair, who was clutching a teddy bear, this had nothing written underneath it. My inspection was interrupted by a voice from behind the curtain. Are you still there?, asked the Porter of the Pensão Isadora. Of course I'm still here, I said. I turned towards the counter and attempted a smile, but the man wasn't smiling. What do you want?, he asked wearily. I want a room, I said, I thought that was obvious. A room?, he repeated, what for? A room to sleep in, I said, I need to sleep. The Porter of the Pensão Isadora stroked his thin moustache, put on a grave face, scratched his bottom and said: This is a serious guesthouse, my friend, we don't take single people here, do I make myself clear? No, you don't, I said stubbornly, explain it to me again. We only take couples, said the Porter of the Pensão Isadora, we don't want any peeping Toms or perverts here. Fine, I said, if that's the problem, look, I've already said that all I want to do is sleep, I need to lie down for a couple of hours on a bed, a nice clean bed. Then why don't you find a decent hotel?, he said, not without a certain logic. Listen, I said, it would take too long to explain, but the fact is that I have to spend the whole day in Lisbon and I haven't got much money, as I told you before, I just want to sleep for a couple of hours, I had a heavy lunch and if I don't have a nap I'll have indigestion all afternoon, I just need to sleep, I don't want to inconvenience anyone. The Porter of the Pensão Isadora seemed unconvinced. He stroked his moustache again and asked me: But what made you come here? I saw that I wasn't going to get anywhere with him, so I said: Is Isadora in? I'd like to talk to her, tell her a friend of hers sent me. The Porter of the Pensão Isadora went to the stairs and shouted: Isadora, come down here, there's a guy wants to talk to you! I heard heavy footsteps along the corridor above and Isadora appeared on the stairs. She was an old prostitute, now retired, who had taken on a rather respectable air, a pair of spectacles hung about her neck on a chain and she wore a scarlet blouse. With all the aplomb of a headmistress, Isadora advanced down the stairs towards me. I do apologise, she said, our porter can be a little rude at times but, you know, with the things that go on nowadays, you can't be too careful, but if you wanted to speak to me, you should have said so at once. Tadeus sent me, I said, I'm a friend of his, he sends his best regards, look, I just wanted a room to rest in for a couple of hours and a nice clean bed, I just wanted to have a nap, I had lunch with Tadeus, we ate *sarrabulho*, and I'm dead on my feet, plus I didn't sleep last night because the farm dog kept barking, and I have to meet someone at midnight on the Cais de Alcântara. My dear boy, said Isadora, you should have said so right away, I'll get a nice cool room ready for you with a clean bed, but why doesn't Tadeus call round any more, damn him? I don't know, I said, I expect he's got problems. Isadora rang the bell on the counter, at the same time calling out: Viriata! Viriata! Then she turned to me again and said: You can have number fifteen, my dear, it's on the first floor, right next to the bathroom, Viriata's just going to make up the bed. Do you need my identity card?, I asked. Certainly not, she said. I went up the stairs and into room fifteen. It was a spacious room, with a large double bed and was furnished with the sort of furniture you find in the provinces: a dresser with capacious drawers, a mirrored wardrobe, a few dark chairs. In one corner, near the window, was a washstand made out of wrought iron with a jug of water on it. I laid my jacket and my spare Lacoste shirt on the dresser and waited for the maid. After a while there was a knock on the door and I said: Come in. Good afternoon, said the woman, I'm Viriata. She was a plump young woman, with a very curly perm and a country face. She couldn't have been more than twenty-five but she looked forty. I'm from the Alentejo, she said smiling, we nearly all are here, apart from one little girl called Mercedes, who's Spanish, but now she only works here every other day, otherwise she works in Praça da Alegria, she wants to be a jazz singer. She began putting the clean sheets on the bed and said:

I'd like to be a singer too, but I've never studied music, Mercedes did, she went to a posh school in Mérida, she comes from a good family. And you, I asked, didn't you study anything? Me, no, she said, I only learned how to read and write, my mother died when I was eight and my father was a pig, always drunk, do you like the Alentejo? Very much, I said, do you know, this very morning I was in the Alentejo, in Azeitão. Oh, she said, Azeitão isn't the real Alentejo, it's practically in Lisbon, to really get the feel of the Alentejo you have to visit Beja and Serpa, I'm from Serpa, when I was a little girl I used to keep sheep near the walls of Serpa and on Christmas Eve, the shepherds used to get together in their houses and sing old folk songs, it was so nice, only the men sang, the women just listened and cooked, we used to eat *migas*, *açorda* and *sargalheta*, the sort of food you don't get in Lisbon any more, Lisbon's gone all posh now, do you know, yesterday I went to have lunch in a little restaurant just next door here, nothing special but the fish is good, I ordered sole and the waiter said to me: Grilled or with bananas? With bananas?, I said, what do you mean, with bananas? It's Brazilian-style, the waiter said to me, and if you didn't know before, now you do. I know, I said, the world's gone mad, with all these peculiar fads, it's a complete mess really. Viriata finished making the bed and folded down the sheet for me. Right, she said, the bed's ready, would you like some company? No thanks, Viriata, I said, I just want to sleep for an hour and a half, I don't need any company. I'm very clean and quiet, Viriata said, even if you want to sleep I won't bother you, I'll just lie next to you really still. Thanks again, I said, but I prefer to sleep alone. How about if I scratched your back?, said Viriata, wouldn't you like to go to sleep with someone scratching your back? I smiled and said: Viriata, thank you, you're a lovely girl, but I don't need anyone to scratch my back, I just want to lie quietly for an hour and a half, I'm sorry, Viriata, but it's not a very good day for me to have my back scratched, but listen, can you come and wake me up in an hour and a half, don't forget now and I'll give you a big tip. Viriata left silently. I lowered the blinds. The room was cool, the bed clean, I calmly got undressed, hung my trousers over the back of a chair, took off the gypsy woman's Lacoste shirt and slid naked into bed, it was good to be there, the pillow was soft. I stretched out my legs and closed my eyes.

How many letters are there in the Latin alphabet?, asked my father's voice. I looked carefully and there in the half-light was my father. He was standing at the far end of the room, leaning on the dresser, watching me mischievously. He was in his sailor's uniform, he looked about twenty-something, but he was definitely my father, there was no mistake about that. Dad, I said, what are you doing here in the Pensão Isadora, dressed as a sailor? What are *you* doing here?, he responded, it's 1932, I'm doing my military service and my ship got into Lisbon today, it's called the *Filiberto*, it's a frigate. But why are you talking to me in Portuguese, Dad?, I said, and why when you appear to me do you always ask me absurd questions?, it's as though you were putting me through an exam, last month you turned up to ask me when my mother was born, I can never remember dates, I get confused, I'm useless with numbers, Dad, but you're always tormenting me with these questions. He said, I just want to see if you're a good son, that's all, that's why I keep asking you questions, to see if you're a good son. My Father as a Young Man took off his sailor's hat and smoothed back his hair. He was good-looking, my Father as a Young Man, he had an honest face and lovely blonde hair. Look Dad, I said, to tell the truth, I don't like these questions, these exams, you've got to stop appearing to me like this, whenever you fancy it, you've got to stop bothering me. Hang on a minute, he said, I'm here because I want to know something, I want to know how my life will end and you're the only one who can know that, you're living in the present, I want to know everything today, Sunday, 30th July 1932. What good will it do you to know?, I said, it won't do you any good at all, life is whatever it's going to be, there's nothing you can do about it, let it be, Dad. No, no, said my Father as a Young Man, I'll forget it the moment I leave the Pensão Isadora, there's a girl waiting for me in Rua da Moeda, as soon as I leave here, I'll forget everything, but I need to know now, that's why I keep bothering you. All right, Dad, if that's what you want, I said, your life ends badly, with cancer of the larynx, which is odd because you never smoked, but anyway, that's how it is, you're going to get cancer, and the surgeon who operates on you is the director of the clinic, a famous otolaryngologist, now there's a word!, but in my opinion, the only thing the guy knows about is tonsils, I don't think he understands a thing about cancer. And then?, asked my Father as a Young Man. And then you stay in the hospital for a month, I spend the nights with you because the nurses in the famous professor's clinic have

49

to pg. 53

other things to do, if you ring the bell no one comes and they leave you there choking like a dog, so I have to be there at your bedside and work the disgusting machine that extracts the blood from your throat, and a month later, the day before you're due to leave hospital, the doctors introduce a small tube through your nose down into your stomach so that they can feed you and they say: Everything's fine now, the patient can go home, but everything isn't fine, I go out for a coffee and when I come back to your room I find you dying, your face is all swollen and purple, you can't breathe, you've got palpitations. What's wrong with my father?, I ask the doctor on duty, a crafty so-and-so. Your father's having a heart attack, he says. Then I want a cardiologist, I say, because I don't believe you. The cardiologist arrives, gives you an electrocardiogram and says: The patient has nothing wrong with his heart but there is something wrong with his lungs, he needs an X-ray. And then I pick you up from the bed in my arms, because the nurses at the famous professor's clinic have other things to do, and I call an ambulance and we go in the ambulance to the X-ray clinic, on my responsibility, because the sly doctor on duty says that you can only leave if I take full responsibility, so I do and the radiologist, after the X-ray, says: A tube has perforated your father's oesophagus, pierced the mediastinum and entered the lung, now you need a specialist in pulmonary diseases with a scalpel, if not, your father will die. You see, Dad, when those eminent doctors introduced the tube into your stomach, they perforated first your oesophagus and then your lung, I took you away because I had no faith in them or in their competence; the specialist, whom I called at once, made an incision in your back with a scalpel, the air was expelled and the lung deflated, they put you in intensive care, that place where all the patients lie there naked connected up by tubes on all sides, and after two weeks you recovered, I should say that during all the time you were there, the famous doctor who had first operated on you never once came to see you, the bastard. And then?, asked my Father as a Young Man, what happened to me then? Well, Dad, I said, then I found a really good surgeon, a friend of mine who works in a big hospital, he performed the anastomosis on you, I mean the reconstruction of your perforated oesophagus, and after that you lived for another three years, three nice, peaceful years, eating normally, but then your illness reappeared, this time the disease had spread, and you died. How?, asked my Father as a Young Man, I want to know how, if it was a painful death or if it was peaceful, how was it?, I want to know. You just burned out like a candle, Dad, I said, one day you lay down and you said: I'm tired and I'm not hungry, and you never got up or ate anything again, apart from the soup that Mum used to make for you, I'd come and visit you every day, and you went on like that for a month, you were little more than a skeleton by then but you weren't in any pain, and when you died, you waved to me before going into the dark.

My Father as a Young Man smiled and smoothed back his hair. But there's another story you should tell me, he said, you haven't finished yet. There's nothing else, I said. Don't be obtuse, he said, I want to know if you were a good son, how you behaved towards the doctor who operated on me. Look, Dad, I said, I don't know if I did the right thing, maybe I should have done things differently, I should have just punched the guy, that would have been a braver solution, but I didn't, that's why I'm left with this feeling of guilt, instead of smashing his face in, I wrote a story about the conversation I'd had with him and he brought a case against me, alleging it was false, I couldn't prove to the judge that what I'd said was true and I lost the case. Were you found guilty?, my Father as a Young Man asked. It's not final yet, I said, I appealed and the trial is still going on, but I wish I'd done it differently, I wish I'd punched him, that would have been honourable, radical, in the old tradition. Don't be hard on yourself, son, said my Father as a Young Man, you did the best thing, it's better to use the pen than brute force, it's a more elegant way of delivering a punch. It's nice of you to comfort me, Dad, I said, because I don't feel satisfied with myself. That's why I'm here in this room, said my Father as a Young Man, because I wanted to reassure you, to reassure us both, now that you've told me everything, I feel more at peace. I hope so, Dad, I hope you don't come back again the way you have done recently, it's frightening, it was becoming unbearable. There's one thing you should know, said my Father as a Young Man, I didn't choose to appear in this room, it was your will that called me here, because it was you who wanted me in your dream, and now I only have time to say goodbye, goodbye my son, the maid is just about to knock on the door, I have to leave.

I heard the knocking on the door and opened my eyes, Viriata came in and said: Good afternoon, you've slept for exactly an hour and a half, I'm very punctual as you see, I hope you've had a good rest. She placed my trousers and my shirt on the edge of the bed and asked: Are you staying here tonight? No, Viriata, I said, I have to leave, I want to go for a walk. In this heat?, asked Viriata, alarmed. It's not a long walk, I said, and I might take the tram, I've got the whole afternoon ahead of me and I want to visit a painting. Visit a painting?, said Viriata, what a weird idea. I never really understood what the painting meant, you see, perhaps today I'll understand it better, who knows, today's a very special day. If you don't mind, then, I'll come with you to the tram stop, said Viriata, I'd like to go for a walk too. With the greatest of pleasure, Viriata, I said, but first hand me the wallet that's in my trouser pocket. Viriata understood at once, raised her hands and exclaimed: Certainly not, I don't want a tip, you've been very kind to me and kindness is the best gift you can give to someone you don't know.

V

YOUR PINEAPPLE *SUMOL*, the Barman at the
Museum of Ancient Art said in a bored voice, placing
the glass on my table. The garden's lovely, I said, just
to say something, it's beautifully cool even on a hot day
like today, it was a good idea to open a café here, the
museum really needed one, in my day there wasn't anything. Right, the Barman said in the same bored tone,
we serve alcoholic drinks and everything, but unfortunately the customers drink nothing but *Sumol* and lemonade. I need a *Sumol* to help my digestion, I said, I had a
rather heavy lunch today, it still hasn't gone down. Alcohol's the best thing for that, said the Barman, it's alcohol
that aids digestion, you're a foreigner you should know
that. Why should a foreigner know about that?, I asked.
Because abroad they know everything, he said implac-
ably, the problem in this country is that people don't
know anything, they're ignorant, they don't travel
enough. Would you like to sit down?, I asked, offering
him a chair. The Barman at the Museum of Ancient Art
looked around. All right, he said, seeing as no one's here
I can rest my legs a bit, I've been on my feet since this
morning. He sat down, crossed his legs and took out a
cigarette. And what about you, have you travelled a lot?,

I asked him, picking up the conversation again. I lived in France, he replied, I worked there for a long time, I lived really well in Paris, but last year I decided to come back and now here I am serving lemonades, I should be working in one of those posh bars in Cascais, the sort of bars where the English and the French go to drink, but I couldn't get a job there, it's almost impossible to get a job in Cascais and Estoril, and I'll tell you something else, there are guys working as barmen there who can't tell a Bourbon from a Macieira brandy, it's pathetic. Don't you like serving people lemonade?, I asked. Well, he said, the thing is I'm a barman by profession, I mean a real barman, the sort who mixes cocktails and long drinks, I'm wasted here, I used to work at Harry's Bar in Paris, perhaps you know it. No, I don't, I said. It's in Rue Daunau, he said, near the Opera, if you're ever passing, pop in and ask for Daniel, you can mention my name, he's the best barman in the world, he taught me everything I know, he's getting on a bit now but he's still the best, just order an "Alexander" and you'll see what I mean. The Barman at the Museum of Ancient Art stubbed out his cigarette in the ashtray and sighed. Quite a change as you can see, he said, now here I am serving nothing but lemonade, do you know, in Harry's Bar we had a hundred and sixty different types of whisky, do you see what I mean?, Harry's Bar is like the *quartier général* of all the English and Americans living in Paris, people who really know how to drink, not like the Portuguese who just drink fruit juice. Rather shamefacedly I finished my *Sumol* and said: I don't agree, I think the Portuguese can drink with the best of them. Wine maybe, said the Barman, as far as wine's concerned you're quite right, I wouldn't disagree with you there, but you see they drink almost nothing else. They drink *grappa*, I said, they don't hold back when it comes to that. I know, said the Barman at the Museum of Ancient Art resignedly, but they don't like cocktails, they haven't a clue about them. So why did you come back?, I said, you could have stayed in Paris. I had to, he sighed again, my mother-in-law got ill, she had a stroke, she was living on her own in Benfica and my wife wanted to take care of her, besides, my wife never really liked France, she missed things like *chouriço* sausage and sardines, my wife's terribly Portuguese, poor woman, but she's a good sort, so what else could I do, and here I am serving people lemonade. The Barman at the Museum of Ancient Art looked at my empty glass and winked at me. Have you digested your meal now?, he asked. Yes, I think so, I said, *Sumol* is wonderful for the digestion, especially pineapple *Sumol*. Then perhaps I can recommend you one of my own concoctions, said the Barman, it's a cocktail I invented when I came to work here, you won't believe who drank it here yesterday, go on, have a guess. I've no idea, I said, not an inkling. You really don't know who was here yesterday?, asked the Barman at the Museum of Ancient Art, disappointed, it was even in the newspapers, *O Público*'s colour supplement gave it a big photo spread, I'm in one of the photos. I didn't buy the morning papers, I said, I'm sorry, I only bought *A Bola*. *A Bola*!, he exclaimed scornfully, you should buy *O Público*, it's more like a French newspaper. I know, I said, but unfortunately I only bought *A Bola*. Oh well, said the Barman at the Museum of Ancient Art, but look, try and guess. Guess what, I asked. Guess who was here yesterday, he said. I don't know, I said, I haven't a clue. The President of the Republic! exclaimed the Barman at the Museum of Ancient Art proudly, the President of the Republic was here in person, he came with a foreign guest who's on an official visit to Portugal, the prime minister of some Asian country, and they came to visit the museum. The Barman slapped me on the back as if we were old friends. Well, he said, I'm not one to boast, but what do you think he said to me?, he said: Good afternoon, Senhor Manuel, can you imagine, he called me by my name, Senhor Manuel. They have a very efficient information service, I said, and before making any visit, they find out about things like that, they know everything. No, that's not what happened at all, sir, objected the Barman at the Museum of Ancient Art, not at all, the fact is that the President of the Republic was once in Harry's Bar, years ago now, when he was in exile in Paris, and he simply remembered my name, he's got a remarkable memory, our president. Really extraordinary, I said, but then that's a fundamental quality in a good politician, a memory like an elephant. The Barman at the Museum of Ancient Art went on: he said, how are you, Senhor Manuel?, don't you think that's amazing? I do, I said, and how did you respond? I shook him by the hand, the Barman said, and I mixed him a good cocktail, because I know he likes a drink, he's a remarkable man, our President, but he likes his food, he enjoys eating and drinking, and so I mixed him a really good drink, the very drink I was recommending to you, wouldn't you like to try it, now that your stomach's settled down a bit? I might, I said, what is it? Look, he said, it isn't exactly a cocktail and it isn't exactly a long drink, let's just say it's something in between, it's a drink I invented, it's called "Janelas Verdes' Dream", after the street the museum's in. Very appropriate, I said, but what's it made of? Look, my friend, said the Barman at the Museum of Ancient Art confidentially, I don't usually reveal the ingredients of any of my creations, they're a professional secret, but you're a foreigner and so I'll tell you, it's three parts vodka to one part lemon juice plus a spoonful of crème de menthe, you put all the ingredients in a shaker with three ice cubes, shake it hard until your arm aches and remove the ice before serving, the vodka and the lemon juice blend perfectly and the crème de menthe gives both the smell and the green colour you need for the name, do you get it?, *verde* as in Janelas Verdes, the colour's absolutely essential. All right, I said, I will try a "Janelas Verdes' Dream", you've convinced me. An excellent choice, exclaimed the Barman at the Museum of Ancient Art, I'll tell you something else, the lemon juice quenches your thirst, the alcohol gives you energy, which you need on a hot day like today, and the peppermint refreshes your insides, an excellent choice. He jumped up and went over to the bar. I looked at the clock and realised it was getting late, I wouldn't have time to see my painting. The Barman at the Museum of Ancient Art returned with my "Janelas Verdes' Dream" and placed the glass on the table with a look of triumph. I raised the glass to my lips and thought that, however ghastly it turned out to be, I couldn't back down, I had to show I was a man, but it wasn't ghastly at all, in fact I smacked my lips and said: It's really good. The Barman sat down again and said: It is, isn't it? It is, I said, it really is. And then I went on: Look, my friend, could you do me a favour?, do you know the museum guards? Every one of them, he said unhesitatingly, they're all friends of mine. Well, look, I said, my problem is this, I came here to see a painting, but I've only just realised that the museum's about to close, I really need to see this painting, but ten minutes won't be enough, I need at least an hour, could you ask the guard who's in charge of that room if I could stay on for an hour? I can try, said the Barman at the Museum of Ancient Art with a conspiratorial look, the staff don't leave until an hour after closing time anyway, because of the cleaners, you might be able to stay on for a while. Then he lowered his voice, as if what he was asking were a secret: Which painting is it? *The Temptation of St Anthony*, I said. Haven't you ever seen it?, he asked. Dozens of times, I said. Then why do you want to see it again, if you've already seen it?, he asked. It's just a whim, I said, let's just call it a whim. That's fine, he said, I understand all about whims, anything to do with whims or alcohol, I'm your man. I asked: Do you think a tip would help to persuade the attendant? No, I think that might be a bit out of order, he said.

He disappeared while I finished my cocktail and set to thinking. I really wanted to see the painting again. How many years was it since I'd last seen it? I tried to work it out but couldn't. Then I remembered those winter afternoons spent in the museum, the four of us, and the conversations we'd had, our meditations on its symbolism, our interpretations, our enthusiasm. And now here I was again and everything was different, only the painting had stayed the same, and it was upstairs waiting for me. But will it have stayed the same or will it have changed too? I mean, isn't it possible that the painting could be different now simply because my eyes would no longer see it in the same way? That was what I was asking myself when the Barman at the Museum of Ancient Art returned. He came over to me very nonchalantly and winked. Right, he said, it's all arranged, the guard is Senhor Joaquim, he's waiting for you. I got up and paid the bill. The cocktail was really delicious, I said, thank you, I feel much better now. The Barman at the Museum of Ancient Art shook my hand. Goodbye, he said, I like people who know how to appreciate cocktails, and remember, if you're ever in Harry's Bar, ask for Daniel and say Manuel sent you.

When I got to the room, the guard gave me a nod of recognition, I thanked him and said I wouldn't be more than an hour, he said not to worry and I went in. To my great disappointment I saw I wasn't alone, for right in front of the painting stood a copyist, with easel and canvas. I don't know why but it displeased me to have company, I would like to have seen the painting on my own without other eyes looking at it, without the slightly discomforting presence of a stranger. It was perhaps because of that feeling of unease that instead of standing in front of the painting, I went round to the other side to study the back of the left-hand panel, the scene that shows Christ being arrested in the Garden. I tried to concentrate on the scene, perhaps in the rather absurd hope that the man would fold up his easel and leave. If you want to see the painting, you'll have to hurry up, said the man from the other side, the museum's about to close. I peered round at him and gave a faint smile.

The guard was kind enough to let me stay another hour, I said. The guards in this museum are all very kind, said the man, don't you think? I came out from behind the painting and went over to him. Are you making a copy?, I asked stupidly. A copy of a detail, he replied, as you can see, that's what I do mainly, details. I looked at the canvas he was working on and saw that he was reproducing a detail from the right-hand panel that depicts a fat man and an old woman travelling through the sky mounted on a fish. The canvas was over six feet across and three feet high, and the effect of blowing up the Bosch figures to that size was most odd: the monstrous size seemed to emphasise the monstrousness of the scene. But what are you doing?, I asked in a shocked voice, what are you doing? I'm copying a detail, he said, can't you see?, I'm simply making a copy of a detail, I'm a copyist and I make copies of details. I'd never seen a detail from a Bosch painting reproduced in those dimensions, I explained, it's monstrous. Perhaps, replied the Copyist, but some people like it. Look, I said, forgive me being nosy, but I don't understand, why do something like that?, it doesn't make sense. The Copyist put down his brush and cleaned his hands on a rag. My dear friend, he said, life is strange and strange things happen in life, besides the painting itself is strange and causes strange things to happen. He took a drink of water from the plastic bottle he'd placed at the foot of the easel and said: I've worked really hard today, I can afford to take a break and have a bit of a chat, you know this painting, are you a critic? No, I said, just an amateur, I've known this painting for years though, there was a time when I used to come and see it every week, it fascinates me. I've been looking at this painting for ten years, said the Copyist, and working on it for ten years. Really?, I said, ten years is a long time, and what have you done in those ten years? I've painted details, said the Copyist, I've spent ten years painting details. It really is strange, I said, forgive me but I do find it strange. The Copyist shook his head. So do I, he said, the whole story started ten years ago, at the time I was working at the Town Hall, in an administrative job, but I did a course at the School of Fine Arts and I always liked painting, I mean, I liked it but I had nothing to paint, I had no inspiration, and inspiration is fundamental to painting. It certainly is, I agreed, without inspiration painting is nothing, the same with the other arts. Well, anyway, said the Copyist, since I had no inspiration but enjoyed painting, I used to come to this museum every Sunday and amuse myself by copying one of the pictures here. He took another swallow of water and went on: One Sunday I set to painting a detail from the Bosch, it was a joke really, it could have been anything, but because I like fish I chose the ray in the central panel, just above the *gryllos*, see?

Gryllos?, I asked, what does that mean? That's what the torso-less creatures Bosch painted are called, said the Copyist, it's an old name that was rediscovered by modern critics like Baltrusaitis, but in fact it's a name that dates from Antiquity, it was Antiphilus who coined the word, because he used to paint creatures like that, creatures without a torso, just a head and arms. The Copyist sat down on the tiny folding seat in front of the painting and said: I'm tired. Then he took out a cigarette and lit it. Joaquim has closed the room now, he said, and I could really do with a cigarette. What happened next?, I asked, you were telling me about the Sunday you painted the ray. Right, he said, I started painting it partly as a joke and partly because I had an idea I could sell it to a restaurant, I'd occasionally sold paintings of fish to A Fortaleza, perhaps you know it, it's a restaurant in Cascais, it does Portuguese and international cuisine, and it has a splendid panoramic view over the bay, I still do the odd painting for them, but much less often now, anyway, it's a fabulous restaurant, they serve a steamed lobster which is out of this world, if you ever go to Cascais make sure you go there. He took a card out of his pocket and gave it to me, it was a card from the restaurant. It's closed on Wednesdays, he added. I looked at the card and asked: Anyway, what about this ray you were painting? Well, he said, I was painting the ray and I'd nearly finished it, it had turned out really well and I was just folding up my easel, when a foreign gentleman who'd been watching me work, came over and said to me in Portuguese: I want to buy your painting, I'll pay you in dollars. I looked at him and I said: I'm sorry, but this painting is for a restaurant in Cascais. *I'm* very sorry, he said, but this painting is going to my ranch in Texas, my name's Francis Jeff Silver and I have a ranch in Texas the size of Lisbon, I have a house without a single painting in it and I'm mad about Bosch, I want that painting for my house. The Copyist stubbed out his cigarette on the floor and said: That's how it all began. I don't understand, I said, how does the story go on? It's simple, he said, the Texan started commissioning more paintings from me, details, what he wanted were enormous copies of details from *The Temptations*, like I said, the Texan has a house full of them, all six feet across, last summer I went there, you know, he invited me over and paid my fare, you can't imagine what it's like, the house is huge, there's a tennis court, two swimming pools and the house itself has got thirty rooms which are almost full now of these vast paintings of details from *The Temptations*. And what about you?, I asked, what will you do now? Well, said the Copyist, I've asked the town hall if I can take early retirement, I'm fifty-five now and I don't enjoy administrative work, the Texan pays me enough to live on and I reckon I've got another good ten years of work to do, he wants details from the panels on the back as well, so I've still got a lot to paint. So you know everything there is to know about this painting, I said. I know this painting like the back of my hand, he said, for example, you see what I'm painting now?, well, all the critics have always said that this fish is a sea bass, but it isn't at all, it's a tench. A tench, I said, that's a freshwater fish, isn't it? It is indeed, he said, it lives in swamps and ditches, it loves mud, it's the greasiest fish I've eaten in my life, where I come from they cook a rice dish made with tench which is just swimming in grease, it's a bit like eels and rice only even greasier, it takes a whole day to digest. The Copyist paused briefly. Anyway, he said, these two characters are off to meet the devil mounted on this greasiest of fish, do you see, they've obviously got some devilish rendezvous, they're certainly up to no good. The Copyist opened a small bottle of turpentine and began carefully cleaning his hands. Bosch had a perverse imagination, he said, he attributes that imagination to poor old St Anthony, but in fact it's the painter's imagination, he was the one who thought up all those ugly things, I don't think St Anthony would ever have imagined them, he was a simple soul. But he was tempted, I pointed out, it's the Devil feeding his imagination with all those perversions, Bosch painted the storm in the saint's soul, what he painted was the saint's delirium. There's something else too, said the Copyist, in the old days this painting was thought to have magical powers, sick people would file past it hoping that some miraculous intervention would put an end to their suffering. The Copyist saw the surprise on my face and asked: Didn't you know that? No, I said, I didn't actually. Well, he said, the painting was on show at the hospital run by the order of St Anthony in Lisbon, it was a hospital that cared for people with skin diseases, mostly venereal in origin, and a ghastly affliction, a sort of epidemic erysipelas, which they used to call St Anthony's Fire, in fact people in the country still call it that, it's a really terrible disease because it appears cyclically and the area it affects becomes covered in horrible blisters, which are really painful, but it has a more scientific name now, it's a virus, it's called herpes zoster. My heart began to beat faster, I became aware I was sweating and I asked: How do you know all this? Don't forget I've been working on this painting for the last ten years, he said, it holds no secrets for me now. Then tell me about this virus, I said, what do you know about it? It's a very strange virus, said the Copyist, it seems that we all harbour it inside us in its larval state, but it only manifests itself when the organism's defences are low, then it attacks with a vengeance, only to go into a dormant state again until the next attack, it's cyclical, you see, I'll tell you something, I think herpes is a bit like remorse, it lies dormant within us and then, one fine day, it wakes up and attacks us, then goes to sleep again, only because we've managed to suppress it, but it's always there inside us, there's no cure for remorse.

The Copyist began putting away his brushes and his palette. He covered the canvas with a cloth and asked me to help him move the easel over against the wall at the back. Right, he said, I think that's enough for today, mustn't overdo it, my client wants the painting by the end of August, I think I'll make it, what do you reckon? I'd say you had loads of time, I replied, you're pretty far advanced, it's almost finished. Will you be much longer?, asked the Copyist. No, I said, I don't think so, I think I've seen enough of this painting, and besides today I've learned things about it I never would have suspected, it has a meaning for me now that it didn't before. I'm off to Rua do Alecrim, said the Copyist. Great, I said, I'm going to Cais do Sodré to catch a train to Cascais, we can walk part of the way together.

VI

"SOMETHING YOU PUT on your finger and the noise the telephone makes?" said the Ticket Collector on the train, any idea what that could be? He sat down opposite me and showed me the crossword puzzle in the newspaper. How many letters?, I asked. Four, he said. "Ring", I said, it must be "ring". Of course! exclaimed the Ticket Collector, I don't know how I didn't get that. Crossword clues are difficult to guess when they use puns or plays on words, I said, they're always the hardest.

The carriage was empty, in fact the whole train appeared to be empty, I must have been the only passenger.

You're lucky to have time to do the crossword, I remarked, there's no one on the train today. Not now, he said, but on the way back it'll be hell. We were passing through Oeiras and he pointed to the beach packed with people. You couldn't see the sand, just bodies, like a huge flesh-coloured stain covering the beach. It'll be hell, he said again, there'll be all kinds of people, boys and girls, cripples, blind people, children and pregnant women, grandfathers and grandmothers, it'll be hell on wheels. Well, I said, that's Sundays for you, everyone goes to the beach. It wasn't like that in my day, said the Ticket Collector, we used to spend our holidays in cool places, we'd go to the country, go back to our villages and visit our parents, that's what we called going on holiday, not any more though, everyone wants to get a tan, they can't get enough of the heat, they spend all day on the beach frying like sardines, and the sun's not good for you, it causes skin cancer, there've been articles about it in the paper, but no one cares. The Ticket Collector sighed and looked out of the window. We were at Alto da Barra and you could see the Torre de Bugio standing in the middle of the sea. They drink Coca-Cola too, he added, they spend all day drinking that muck, I don't know if you've ever been on Oeiras beach on a Monday morning, but it's covered in *caricas*, like a carpet. *Caricas?*, I said, I don't know that word. Bottle tops, said the Ticket Collector, *caricas* is what country people call them. Oh, I said. And then I asked: Do you mind if I smoke?, there's no one else on the train. Feel free he said, smoke all you want, I'll have one too. We both reached for our packs of cigarettes at the same time, I offered him one of mine and he offered me one of his. What do you smoke?, the Ticket Collector asked. Multifilter, I replied, you can't buy them in Portugal, they're very mild, it's almost like inhaling air, it says on the packet "activated charcoal filtration system", which means it hasn't got much nicotine or tar, but it's still rubbish, smoking causes cancer too, it's worse than the sun. Everything causes cancer, replied the Ticket Collector, even being unhappy, I had a friend who died of cancer because he wasn't happy. He took the cigarette I was holding out to him and gave me one of his. I smoke

Português Suave, he said, I used to smoke Definitivos, but you hardly ever see them now, people's tastes have changed completely, even in cigarettes.

I would like to have closed my eyes for a few minutes, but he went on chatting. We were passing São Pedro and he pointed something out to me. Can you imagine building anything more horrible than that?, he said indicating the houses you could see through the opposite window, have you ever seen anything uglier? They're certainly ugly, I said, but who allowed such monstrosities to be built? I don't know, said the Ticket Collector, I don't know, the local councils in Portugal are a law to themselves, they take on architects who are like kids playing with Lego, they're all a bunch of incompetents really, who want more than anything else to be modern. I get the impression you don't much like anything modern, I said. I hate it, he said, it's hideous all of it, good taste is basically fucked, if you'll pardon the expression, you just have to look at the miniskirt, horrible don't you think?, a young girl can get away with it, but on fat women, with those great knees of theirs, it looks really revolting, it takes away a woman's charm, takes away their mystery. He looked down at his crossword puzzle again and said: Here we are, here's a bit of modernity for you: "Modern architect – singer with a stutter"? It's got five letters. Aalto, I said, he was a Finnish architect, Alvar Aalto. Aalto, he said, I doubt he was any good. On the contrary, I said, he more or less rebuilt Helsinki in the fifties and designed some other really lovely houses in other parts of Europe too, I like his work. Have you been to Helsinki?, the Ticket Collector asked. I have, I said, it's an odd city, all in brick and with these buildings designed by Aalto and it's surrounded by forests. What about the people?, he asked, what are they like? They read a lot and they drink a lot, I said, they're good people, I like people who know how to drink. So you like the Portuguese then, he said, not entirely illogically.

The train was just entering Cascais. Nice, eh?, said the Ticket Collector indicating the Estoril Sol. Modern, I replied, so modern it's already out of date. And then I asked: Do you think a taxi as far as the road to Guincho will cost more than five hundred *escudos*? I shouldn't think so, he said, taxis are still cheap in Portugal, as a foreigner you should know that, look, I'll tell you something, the only time I left Portugal was to go to Switzerland to visit my son who lives in Geneva, he lives outside the city so I caught a taxi and the taxi fare used up all the money I'd brought with me from Portugal, by the way, are *you* Swiss? Swiss?!, I exclaimed, do you mind? no, I'm Italian. But you're practically Portuguese, he said, I suppose you've lived here for a long time. No, I said, but I must have some Portuguese ancestor I don't know about, I think Portugal's imprinted on my genetic baggage. Genetic baggage?, repeated the Ticket Collector, I've seen that expression in the *Diário de Notícias*, it's that thing with the signs, the plus sign and the minus sign, isn't that it? More or less, I said, but to be honest, I don't really know what genetic baggage is either, I think it means something like nature or character, it would be simpler to call it that. I like the word nature, said the Ticket Collector, my wife always says I'm good-natured, what do you think? I think you're extremely good-natured, I said, and I've really enjoyed talking to you, without this chat my journey would have been very boring.

The old woman appeared at the door and looked at me suspiciously. Good afternoon, I said, I've come to see the house, I'd like to visit it, if you don't mind that is. My house?, asked the old woman, alarmed and uncomprehending. No, I said, not your house, the big house, the one next to the lighthouse. It's all locked up, said the old woman patiently, no one lives there, it's been closed for years now. I know, I said, that's why I wanted to see it, I've come all the way from Lisbon just for that, look, I've got a taxi waiting for me. I pointed to the taxi parked on the other side of the road to prove to her that what I was saying was true. The house is all locked up, she repeated, I'm sorry, but the house is locked up. Are you the housekeeper?, I asked. No, she said, I'm the lighthousekeeper's wife, but when I have time I also take care of the house, I open the windows now and then and do some dusting, here by the sea everything falls to bits, windows, furniture, and the owners don't care, they don't live here, they live abroad, they're Arabs. Arabs?!, I exclaimed, this house belongs to Arabs now? That's right, said the Lighthousekeeper's Wife, the last owner, who'd bought it for next to nothing from the old owners, wanted to build a hotel here, but his company went bust, it seems he was some kind of con man, at least that's what my husband says, so he sold it to the Arabs. Arabs, I repeated, I would never have imagined that one day this house would be owned by Arabs. The whole country's up for grabs, said the Lighthousekeeper's Wife, foreigners are buying up everything, you know. Yes, I said, unfortu-

To pg. 80

nately, but what are these Arabs going to do with the house? Well, said the Lighthousekeeper's Wife, to tell you the truth, I think they're waiting for it to fall down of its own accord, at the moment the council won't give permission to build a hotel, but if it falls down, that's different, they can build something new then. Is it falling down?, I asked. Well, said the Lighthousekeeper's Wife, in April, when we had those storms, the roof collapsed and made a hole in the ceiling in two of the rooms, the rooms facing the sea are in a terrible state, I think that come this winter, the whole top floor will cave in. That's why I came, I said, to see the house before it fell down. Are you interested in buying?, asked the Lighthousekeeper's Wife. No, I said, I don't quite know how to explain, but a long time ago I lived here for a whole year, it was before you worked here. That must have been before 1971 then, she said, that's when we arrived, Vitalina and Francisco must have been here then. Yes, I remember Vitalina and Francisco well, I said, they were around the year I was here, Vitalina looked after the house and did the cooking, she made the best *arroz de tamboril* I've ever had, what happened to them? Francisco died of cirrhosis of the liver, said the Lighthousekeeper's Wife, he used to drink a lot, he was a cousin of my husband, and Vitalina's living with her son now in Cabo da Roca. The whole family are lighthousekeepers, I said. Yes, she said, the whole family, Vitalina's son is lighthousekeeper at Cabo da Roca, but he's earning good money, I think Vitalina's much better off now than when Francisco was alive, she had a terrible time with him, he was always drunk, sometimes she had to go up to the lighthouse herself because he wasn't in a fit state to. I know, I said, one night she came to ask me for help, it was a terrible night, rainy and misty, Francisco was drunk in bed and Vitalina came to wake me up, she wanted to turn on the radio but she couldn't get it to work, so she came and woke me, I spent the whole night with her in the lighthouse. Poor Vitalina, said the Lighthousekeeper's Wife, she had a hard life, it's a real tragedy when all a man thinks about is drink. But Francisco was a nice man, I said, I think he loved his wife. Oh, he loved her all right, said the Lighthousekeeper's Wife, he never hit her, but that didn't stop him getting paralytic every night.

The taxi driver sounded his horn, wanting to know what I intended to do. I signalled to him to wait and said to the Lighthousekeeper's Wife: You don't want to show me the house then? Oh, all right, she said, but we'll have to be quick, my son will be here soon with his family, it's my little granddaughter's birthday today and I have to finish making the supper. That's fine by me, I said, I've got to get the train in Cascais, I have to be in Lisbon at nine o'clock. The Lighthousekeeper's Wife disappeared inside the house. She came back with a bunch of keys and told me to follow her. We crossed the yard to the porch. This is the way in now, she said, I expect when you were here, you used to go in through the French windows on the terrace, but they can't be used any more, the glass is all broken. We went in and I immediately recognised the smell of the house. It smelled a bit like the metro in Paris in winter, a mixture of mustiness, varnish and mahogany, a smell peculiar to that house, and my memories all came back to me. We went into the large sitting room and I saw the piano. It was covered with a sheet, but I still had the urge to sit down at it.

Excuse me, I said, but there's something I must play, I'll be quick, I don't really know how to play properly but anyway. I sat down and with one finger, from memory, I played the melody from a nocturne by Chopin. Other hands, in other times, used to play that melody. I remembered those nights, when I was upstairs in my room, and I would lie listening to Chopin nocturnes. They were solitary nights, the house in winter was swathed in mist, my friends were in Lisbon and didn't come to visit, no one came, no one phoned, I was writing and wondering why I was writing, the story I was working on was a strange story, a story without a solution, what had made me want to write a story like that?, how did I come to be writing it? More than that, the story was changing my life, would change it, once I'd written it, my life would never be the same again. That's what I would say to myself, closeted upstairs writing that strange story, a story that someone afterwards would imitate in real life, would transfer back to the plane of reality. I didn't know that, but I imagined it, I don't know why, but I sensed that one shouldn't write stories like that, because there's always someone who'll try and imitate fiction, who'll manage to make it come true. And that was what happened. That same year someone imitated my story, or rather, the story became flesh, was transubstantiated, and I had to live that crazy story all over again, but this time for real, this time the characters inhabiting the story weren't made of paper, they were flesh and blood, this time the development, the sequence of events in my story unravelled day by day, I followed its progress on the calendar, to the point that I knew what would happen.

Was it a good year?, the Lighthousekeeper's Wife asked me, I mean, were you comfortable here in this house? It was a bewitched year, I replied, there was some kind of witchcraft going on. Do you believe in witches?, asked the Lighthousekeeper's Wife, people like yourself don't usually, they think it's just popular superstition. Oh, I believe, I said, at least in some forms of witchcraft, you know, you should never try to influence things by suggestion, if you do, things end up happening that way. I went to see a clairvoyant when my son was in the war in Guinea Bissau, said the Lighthousekeeper's Wife, I was terribly worried because I'd had a dream, I dreamed that he would never come back, so I talked to my husband and said: Look, Armando, you've got to give me some money because I want to go to the clairvoyant, I had a bad dream, I dreamed that Pedro would never come back and I want to know whether he will or not, anyway, I went to the woman and she laid out the cards, then she turned one card over and said: Your son will come back, but he'll be maimed, and Pedro did come back, but he'd lost an arm. The Lighthousekeeper's Wife opened a door and said: This is the dining room, was this where you used to have supper?

The dining room was exactly as it had been: the fireplace, the sideboard, the Indo-Portuguese furniture, the large, dark-wood table. It was indeed, I said, I used to sit here, in this chair, a woman friend used to sit to my right and, here and here, two other friends of mine. Did Vitalina serve at table?, asked the Lighthousekeeper's Wife. She did, I said, or rather, she brought the things from the kitchen and left them on a tray in the middle of the table and we served ourselves, Vitalina didn't like to serve at table, she preferred the kitchen, apart from *arroz de tamboril* she made a magnificent *açorda de mariscos*, but her speciality was *sopa alentejana*. Because she was from the Alentejo, remarked the Lighthousekeeper's Wife, that's why she could do *sopa alentejana*. You know, my day today has been full of people from the Alentejo, I said, I've just realised that almost everyone I've met today has been from there. *Alentejanos* are very proud, remarked the Lighthousekeeper's Wife, but I like them, I mean, they're nothing like me, I'm from Viana do Castelo and I'm a very different type of person, but I still like them. The Lighthousekeeper's Wife wiped the layer of dust off the sideboard with her apron. Would you like to see upstairs too?, she asked. If you wouldn't mind, I said. Be careful on the stairs, she said, they're very slippery because the wood's so worn, I'll go first.

I opened the door of the room, looked up and saw the sky. It was a very blue sky, transparent, it dazzled the eyes. It was unreal, that room with the bed, the wardrobe and the bedside tables, and almost no roof over it. It's dangerous here, said the Lighthousekeeper's Wife, that one last bit of roof could fall any minute, we can't stay in here. Just for a second, I said, it's not going to fall right now. I stretched out on the bed and said: I'm sorry but I just have to lie down for a moment, as a way of saying goodbye, it's the last time I'll ever lie on this bed. Seeing me lying there, the Lighthousekeeper's Wife discreetly left the room and I stared up at the sky. It was very odd, when I was younger I'd always thought of that blue as mine, as something that belonged to me, but now it seemed exaggerated, distant, like a hallucination, and I thought: It can't be true, it just can't be true that I'm lying here on this bed again and instead of looking up at the ceiling, as I did on so many nights, I'm looking up at a sky that once belonged to me. I got up and went to find the old woman, who was waiting for me in the corridor. One last thing, I said, there's just one other room I'd like to see. There's no guestroom any more, she said, when the roof fell in, everything was ruined, my husband took all the furniture out. I'd just like a look, I said. But you can't go in, she said, my husband says even the floor is dangerous. She opened the door and I peered in. There was nothing in the room and the roof had disappeared completely. You could see the lighthouse through the window. My husband's up there, she said, but he's probably asleep now, there's nothing to do at this hour, but he's so stubborn, and instead of coming home for a sleep, he goes and sleeps in the lighthouse. Do you know what I used to do with that lighthouse in the old days?, I said, I'll tell you, I used to play a game sometimes, when I couldn't sleep, I'd come into this room and stand at the window, the lighthouse has three intermittent lights, one white, one green and one red, and I used to play a game with the lights, I'd invented a luminous alphabet and I used to speak through the lighthouse, as it were. And who were you speaking to?, asked the Lighthousekeeper's Wife. Well, I said, I used to speak to certain invisible presences, I was writing a story at the time, I suppose you could say I was speaking to ghosts. Oh my God, exclaimed the Lighthousekeeper's Wife, weren't you afraid of talking to ghosts? I should never have done it, I said, it's not a good idea to talk to ghosts, you shouldn't do it, but sometimes you have to,

I can't explain it really, but that's partly why I'm here today.

The Lighthousekeeper's Wife had started going down the stairs and turned to tell me to be careful. We went out into the courtyard and she closed the door. Thanks ever so much, I said, take care and say hello to your husband. Would you like something to drink, she said, I've got some cherry brandy, I made it myself. All right, I said, only one glass, though, but it will have to be quick, I'm afraid, I've got to catch the train to be back in Lisbon by nine.

VII

"ALENTEJANOS FOR THE ALENTEJO and the Alentejo for the Fatherland" said the inscription above the door. I went up the wide staircase and emerged into a Moorish courtyard with a small fountain, a glass door and some marble columns lit by red lights, like the lights they use in sacristies. It had a slightly absurd beauty and only then did I understand why I'd arranged to meet Isabel there: precisely because it was such an absurd place. I walked on and, beyond, I saw a reading room, with small tables and newspapers threaded onto wooden poles, like in an English gentleman's club. But there was no one in the room. I looked at my watch and realised that I still had plenty of time before my appointment. I walked slowly across the courtyard. I saw several doors and opened one at random. It opened on to a vast panelled room, eighteenth-century in style, with great glass doors crowned by half-moons painted with frescos. It was the dining room, of monumental size, with all the tables laid and an immense, polished parquet floor. On one side of the room there was a miniature theatre with a tiny red velvet curtain that drew back to reveal a space framed by two columns and dominated by two caryatids carved in yellow wood, two naked figures which, for some reason,

I found indecent, perhaps because they really were. I closed the dining room door and returned to the courtyard. The night was hot, close, like a breath of warm air full of the seaweed smell of the sea. I opened another door and entered the billiard room. It was a large, cool room, its walls lined with fabric. A man, in black jacket and bow tie, was playing billiards on his own. When he saw me, he stopped, rested his cue on the floor and said: Good evening, and welcome. Are you a member?, I asked. The man smiled, rubbed chalk on the tip of the cue and replied: What about you? Are you a member? Me, no, I said, I'm just a visitor, a guest. This club is for members only, he said, I'm the manager, but you were quite right to come in, no one's been in all day, I've spent the whole day alone here, so it's good to see another human being at last.

He was a very small man in his sixties, white-haired and elegant, he had pale eyes and a pleasant face. I arranged to meet someone here at nine o'clock, I said, it was a stupid thing to do, since I'm not a member and I've never been here before, and the person who's coming here belongs only in my memory. The Manager of the Casa do Alentejo rested the cue on the table and smiled a melancholy smile. There's nothing wrong with that, he said, you'll feel perfectly at home here, this club is nothing but a memory, now. Forgive my asking, I said, but what does all this have to do with the Alentejo? The Manager of the Casa do Alentejo smiled again and said: It's a long story, this club was founded by Alentejo landowners, people with land and money who fancied giving a European slant to their lives, they imagined Lisbon was like London and Paris; in the old days, before you were born, they all used to come here to play billiards with their foreign friends, drink port and play billiards, things were different then, this place isn't the same now, the membership's changed but not the club, some of the old *alentejanos* turn up occasionally, but not often, this is a place for memories now. The Manager of the Casa do Alentejo smiled his melancholy smile again. If you want to have supper here, there's not much to choose from, he said, the cook has only made one dish today, it's very good though, *ensopada de borreguinho à moda de Borba*. Thanks, I said, but I'm not sure I'll be eating here, besides I'm not very hungry yet, I might just have a drink, but not right now. I see you're not a great fan of Alentejo cooking, he said. On the contrary, I replied, I love the way they cook game and poultry in the Alentejo, in Elvas once, I had some stuffed turkey, which was simply out of this world, the best turkey I've ever eaten in my life. I couldn't agree more, said the Manager, but I prefer the soups myself, I don't know if you like *poejada* or not, there are two ways of making it, one is with soft cheese and the other is with eggs, which is how they make it in south of the Alentejo, that's where I'm from, whenever I think about my childhood, I always think of the *poejada* my grandmother used to make, our cook makes it too, but you know, here in the city things turn out differently, the food is always more sophisticated, it's nothing like a real *poejada*, it's a soup for posh people. I think it's because the things we remember from our child-hood never return, I said. You're right, he said, there's no point in deluding ourselves.

The Manager of the Casa do Alentejo put more chalk on his cue. Do you like playing bar billiards?, he asked.

I do, I said. Then why don't we play a game?, he said. You're on, I said, but only a quick one, I'd like to wait in the bar for the person who's coming here to meet me. The Manager handed me a cue, carefully set up the pins and said: Let's play the way people used to play, now everyone does it the American way, using huge billiard balls, a terrible game I think. I agree, I said.

The Manager of the Casa do Alentejo played the opening shot and again rubbed chalk on the end of his cue. He played precisely, scientifically, weighing up the state of play with a swift, geometric glance. He was economical in his movements, keeping them to a minimum: a slight lift of the elbow, a slight shift of the shoulder, though still barely moving either arm or shoulder. I see you're a professional, I said, I've obviously got myself into deep water here. He gave another melancholy smile. That's what my life's become, he said, endless solitary afternoons here, playing bar billiards on my own.

I saw that I was in a difficult position. The smallest ball lay exactly midway between my ball and his, it was an impossible shot, which would require either some sort of juggling feat or a huge stroke of luck. I lit a cigarette and studied the situation. I think I've had it, I said, but I'm not giving up just yet, am I allowed to use a screw shot? The use of screw shots is allowed, said the Manager of the Casa do Alentejo ironically, but if you rip the baize you'll have to pay for it. OK, I said, I think I'll have a go anyway. I calmly smoked my cigarette and walked round to the other side of the billiard table to get another perspective on the trajectory my ball would have to follow. I'd like to propose something to you, said the Manager of the Casa do Alentejo. I looked at him, laid my billiard cue down on the table and took off my jacket. Go on, I said. We should place a bet on this shot, he said, I've got a bottle of 1952 port and it's high time I opened it, so if you win it's on me, if you lose, it's on you. I made rapid calculations as to how much a 1952 bottle of port was likely to cost and how much money I had left in my pocket: I really was in no position to be placing bets, I couldn't afford it. The Manager of the Casa do Alentejo gave me a challenging look. Aren't you up to it?, he said. I am, I said. There's nothing I'd like better tonight than to drink a 1952 port. Then if you'll excuse me, he said, and he went off to get the bottle. I sat down in an armchair and went on smoking. I would have liked to do some thinking, but I wasn't in the mood. All I wanted was to be there, smoking, studying the billiard table and the strange geometric pattern the balls had created on the green cloth and from which I had to extricate myself. And the peculiar path my ball would have to follow in order to strike my opponent's ball seemed to me a sign: it was clear that the impossible parabola I would have to achieve on the billiard table was the same parabola I was following that night, and so I made a bet with myself, well not a bet exactly, more of a conjuration, an exorcism, a plea to fate, and I thought: If I manage it, Isabel will appear, if I don't, I'll never see her again.

The Manager of the Casa do Alentejo returned bearing a silver tray with a bottle and two glasses on it and put it down next to the billiard table. Now then, he said, I think we should drink a glass of port before you attempt your shot, I'm sure you could do with a pick-me-up. He opened the bottle precisely, efficiently, and carefully wiped the mouth with a napkin to remove any fragments of cork clinging to the glass. He filled the glasses and held out the tray to me. He was clearly an expert, the Manager of the Casa do Alentejo, but his professionalism seemed out of place in a situation that called for a certain spirit of complicity, affability or even collusion. There wasn't a trace of this in his behaviour or in his attitude, rather there was a professional politeness that underscored the tension of the moment. He raised his glass and I said: Listen, I've actually made two bets, a real one with you and a personal one with myself, would you mind if we drank to the latter? To your own personal wager, then, he said gravely, adding: I've wanted to open this bottle for ages, but it never seemed the right moment.

It was a magnificent port, slightly rough and intensely aromatic. The Manager of the Casa do Alentejo filled the glasses again and said: One more drink, I think the occasion demands it. Have you worked here long?, I asked. Five years, he said, but before that I worked at the Tavares Restaurant, I've spent my life amongst the wealthy, it's awful always living alongside the rich when you're not rich yourself, because you pick up their way of thinking but you can't actually join in, I'd have no problem living the way the rich do because I share their way of thinking, but I haven't the means to do so, only the right mentality. That's definitely not enough, I said. Anyway, today I'm going to drink this port despite them, continued the Manager of the Casa do Alentejo, I'm thoroughly pissed off, if you'll forgive the expression. Not at all, I said, you're perfectly entitled to feel pissed off. Do you know what my trouble is?, he said, it's that I've never allowed myself to feel pissed off, I was always

86

worried about this or that, about the rich, how they were feeling, if they had everything they needed, if they had enough to eat and drink, if they were happy, good God, the rich always have everything they need, they always eat and drink well, they're always happy, I'm a fool to have always worried about them, but I'm going to change my attitude now, I'm going to change my way of thinking, they're rich and I'm not, that's what I have to remember, I have nothing in common with them, even if I have lived in their world, there's no common ground between us. That's what they call class consciousness, I said, at least I think it is. I don't know about that, he said thoughtfully, that's some sort of political label and I don't know much about politics, I never had time for it, I was always too busy working.

The Manager of the Casa do Alentejo filled our glasses again and anxiously raised his to his lips. Forgive that little outburst, he said, I'm sorry. There's no need to apologise, I said, the odd outburst does you good, it helps to detoxify you, besides, class consciousness is very simple, you just came to the realisation that you don't belong to the same class as the rich, it's elementary. And I'll tell you something else, he said, next time I'm not going to vote for their party, I've voted for them ever since the 1974 revolution, you see, I thought of myself as one of them and so I voted for their party, but the game's over, I'm going to change my vote now that I've got class consciousness, do you really think I have? I do, I said, to calm him down, I think you've achieved genuine class consciousness, albeit a little late. Better late than never, he sighed, and filled our glasses again. Not too much, I said, it's very strong this wine and I need quick reflexes for my screw shot. He smiled his melancholy smile and lit a cigarette. Do you mind if I smoke?, he asked. Feel free, I said.

We fell silent, sitting in the armchairs. From far off, outside, came the sound of an ambulance siren. There's someone who's worse off than us, said the Manager of the Casa do Alentejo philosophically, and then he asked: Which party do you think I should vote for? That's a difficult question, I said, I couldn't advise you on anything so personal. But you understand my problem, he said, perhaps you could make a suggestion. Look, I said, if you really have to choose a party, choose according to the dictates of your heart, make a sentimental choice, or rather a visceral one, they're always the best ones. He smiled and said: thank you, I really think it's high time I did something like that, I'm sixty-five years old and if I don't make a visceral choice now, when will I? He replaced the cork in the bottle and said: What's left goes to the winner, I think it's time for you to try your screw shot.

We got up and I noticed that my legs felt a bit unsteady, I thought that in that state it would be a miracle if I managed to hit the ball, nevertheless I picked up my cue, chalked the end and went over to the billiard table. I stood on tiptoe in order to hit the ball from above. My hand was trembling slightly, I really needed a rest, but the screw shot is played without a rest, hitting from above downwards. Perfect silence reigned in the room. I thought: It's now or never, I closed my eyes and hit the ball. The ball began to spin, reached almost the middle of the table, brushing dangerously close to the pins, and then, as if by a miracle, it turned, curved, and very slowly, as if following a prescribed course, touched my opponent's ball and stayed there. You won, said the Manager of the Casa do Alentejo, amazed, that shot deserves a round of applause. He laid his cue down on the table and clapped politely. At that moment, the door-bell rang. He excused himself and went to answer it. I wiped the sweat from my brow with a handkerchief and wondered if this might be the moment to change my shirt again, since I was once more drenched in sweat. I pulled off the shirt I was wearing, placed it on the arm-chair and put on the other blue shirt that I'd been carrying under my arm all day.

There's a lady here asking for you, said the Manager of the Casa do Alentejo when he returned, she says her name's Isabel. Would you show her into the bar, please, I said, I'll be there in a minute. And I picked up the bottle of port.

VIII

THE NIGHT IS HOT, the night is long, a magnificent
night for listening to stories, said the man who came to
sit down next to me on the pedestal beneath the statue
of Dom José. It really was a magnificent night, the moon
was full, the air was warm and soft, there was something
sensual, magical about it. There were scarcely any cars
in the square, the city seemed to have come to a halt,
people had obviously stayed longer than usual at the
beaches and would return later, Terreiro do Paço was
deserted. A ferryboat bound for Cacilhas sounded its siren
before leaving, its lights were the only lights you could
see on the Tagus, everything else was utterly still, as if
caught in a spell. I looked at the man who had spoken
to me, he looked like a tramp, he was very thin and was
wearing tennis shoes and a yellow T-shirt, he had a long
beard and was almost bald, he must have been about my
age or slightly older, he looked at me and raised one arm
in a theatrical gesture. This is the moon of poets, he said,
of poets and storytellers, tonight is an ideal night for
listening to stories, and for telling them too, wouldn't
you like to hear a story? Why should I?, I asked, I can't
see any reason to. The reason is simple, he replied,
because tonight there's a full moon and because you're

here alone watching the river, your soul is lonely and filled with longing, and a story might bring you some happiness. My whole day has been full of stories, I said, I don't think I need any more. The man crossed his legs, rested his chin meditatively on his hands and said: We always need a story even when we think we don't. But why do you want to tell me a story?, I asked, I don't understand. Because I sell stories, he said, I'm a seller of stories, that's my job, I sell the stories that I invent. I still don't understand, I said. Look, he said, that's a long story but not the one I want to tell you tonight, I don't really like talking about myself, I like talking about my characters. No, no, I protested, I find your story very interesting, tell me more about yourself. It's simple, said the Seller of Stories, I'm a failed writer, that's my story. I'm sorry, I said, but I still don't understand, couldn't you tell me more? All right, he said, I'm a doctor, I studied medicine, but medicine wasn't the science I wanted to study, when I was a student I spent my nights writing stories, then I graduated and started work as a doctor, I joined a practice, but I got bored with my patients, I wasn't interested in their cases, what interested me was sitting at my table and writing stories, because I have a prodigious imagination, which is completely unstoppable, it takes me over and forces me to invent stories, all kinds of stories, tragic, comic, dramatic, jolly, superficial, profound, and when my imagination breaks loose, I feel as if I can barely live, I start to sweat, I feel ill, I feel restless, I feel odd, all I can think about are my stories, there's no room for anything else.

The Seller of Stories paused for a moment and repeated the theatrical gesture with his arm, as if he wanted to seize hold of the moon. So what happened?, I asked. One day, he said, I decided to write down the stories that came to me, and so I wrote ten stories, one tragic, one comic, one tragicomic, one dramatic, one sentimental, one ironic, one cynical, one satirical, one fantastic and one realistic and I took the resulting bundle of papers to a publisher. There I met the literary editor of the publishing house, a very sporty young man who wore jeans and chewed gum. He said he would read the whole thing and that I should come back in a week. I went back a week later and the literary editor said: You obviously haven't read any American minimalism, I'm sorry, but you really should have read some American minimalists. I didn't want to admit defeat and so I went to another publisher. There I met a very elegant lady, who wore a scarf round her neck, and she too asked me to come back in a week and so I did. There's too much plot in your stories, the elegant lady told me, you obviously haven't read any avant-garde writers, the avant-garde did away with plot completely, creating plots is positively retrograde now. I still didn't want to admit defeat and so I went to a third publisher. There I met a very serious gentleman who smoked a pipe, he asked me to come back in a week and so I did. You have absolutely no sense of pragmatism, this very serious gentleman told me, your reality is completely fragmented, what you need is a psychiatrist. I left him and started wandering about the city. My practice had closed down, no one went there any more, I was sad and penniless, but even though I was sad, I still had an immense desire to tell my stories to people, and so I started walking and I thought: If I have all these stories to tell, maybe there are people who'd like to hear them, it's a big city, and so I started wandering the city and telling stories, and now that's how I earn my living.

The Seller of Stories lowered his arm and held out a hand to me as if he were offering me something. I give you tonight's moon, he said, and I give you whatever story you feel like hearing, I know you want to hear a story. Yes, I would like to hear a story now, I said, I really would, but it can't be a very long one, I'm meeting someone in a little while on the Cais de Alcântara and I wouldn't want to be late. No problem, said the Seller of Stories, all you have to do is choose the kind of story you'd like to hear tonight. Look, I said, could I just ask you for a bit of information first?, I'd like to invite this person I'm meeting to supper, you must know the city well, perhaps you could tell me the name of a reasonable restaurant near the Cais do Alcântara. There is one, said the Seller of Stories, right opposite the quay, it used to be a station or something, but now it's a kind of social club, it's got a restaurant, a bar, a disco and who knows what else, it's very trendy, I think it's what's called post-modern. Post-modern?, I said, post-modern in what sense? I'm not sure I could explain, said the Seller of Stories, I mean that it's been done up in lots of different styles, for example, the restaurant is full of mirrors and the food they serve is sort of unclassifiable, I mean, it's a place that broke with tradition by embracing tradition, you could describe it as a compilation of several different styles, that's what I would call post-modern. It sounds like the ideal place for my guest, I said, and then I asked: Is it expensive?, it's just that I haven't got much money on me and I'd also like to hear one of your stories, but

I don't know if I can afford it. It isn't expensive, said the Seller of Stories, as long as you don't order smoked swordfish or oysters, because it's a fairly up-scale restaurant and you can get things like that there, but it won't be expensive and, besides, my stories are cheap, since it's late and given your situation, I can offer you a special price, anyway my stories are all different prices, depending on the genre. So what stories have you got to tell me tonight?, I asked. Well, he said, I've got a rather sentimental one that might bring you comfort on a night such as this. I don't want anything sentimental, I said, my whole day has been extremely sentimental and I'm up to here with it. I also have a very funny story, he said, a story that will make you roar with laughter. That's no good either, I said, I don't feel like roaring with laughter. The Seller of Stories sighed. You're very hard to please, he said. Look, I said, just tell me what you've got on offer and how much each story costs. I have a dream story for two hundred *escudos,* he said, a really bizarre one. No, that won't do, I said, I don't want anything bizarre, my whole day has been bizarre in the extreme. And finally, I have a children's story for three hundred *escudos,* he said, the sort of story people used to tell their children to send them to sleep, it's not exactly a fairy story but it tells of a magical world, of a mermaid who used to work in a circus and who fell in love with a fisherman from Ericeira, it's a really nice story, a bit melancholy, with a sad ending that will make you cry. All right, my friend, I said, perhaps I need to cry a bit tonight, tell me the story about the mermaid, I'm going to close my eyes and listen as if I were a child about to fall asleep.

The ferry coming back from Cacilhas sounded its siren as it came alongside the quay. The night really was magnificent, with the moon hanging so low over the arches of Terreiro do Paço that you felt you could have reached out your hand and caught hold of it. I lit a cigarette and settled down to watch the moon and the Seller of Stories began his story.

IX

THE WAITER HAD his hair tied back in a small pony-tail, he was wearing a pair of extremely tight trousers and a pink shirt. I'm Mariazinha, he said with a brilliant smile and then, addressing my guest, he asked: You haven't got anything against people like me, have you? My Guest looked Mariazinha up and down and asked me in English: *Is he mad?* No, I said, I don't think so, he's gay. *Can homosexuals be gay?*, asked my Guest, *what is all this about?* But Botto* was gay, I said, you should know that, you were his friend. *Botto wasn't gay*, he said, *he was an aesthete, it's not the same thing at all.*

Is your friend English? Mariazinha asked me, I can't cope with the English, they're so boring! No, I said, my guest isn't English, he's Portuguese but he lived in South Africa, he likes speaking English, he's a poet. That's all right then, said Mariazinha, I love people who can speak other languages, I can speak Spanish, I learned it in Estremoz, I worked at the Pousada Santa Isabel, *¿les gusta Estremoz, caballeros?* My Guest looked at Mariazinha

---

* António Botto (1897–1959), aesthete and poet. He was the author of the poems *Canções* (*Songs*) (1921), which caused a scandal in Portugal because of their blatantly homosexual content.

again and said: *He's mad.* No, I said, I don't think he is, I'll explain later. Anyway here's the wine list, said Mariazinha, the menu's all here in my little head, I'll tell you what there is later when you're ready to order, I'll leave you now, *caballeros*, I have to see to that big boy all by himself over there, he must be dying of hunger.

Mariazinha walked off, hips swaying, to attend to the needs of a gentleman sitting on his own at a corner table. Where have you brought me?, asked my Guest, what sort of place is this? I don't know, I said, it's the first time I've been here, someone recommended it to me, it's supposed to be post-modern, and if you'll forgive me, you may be partly to blame for all this, I mean for post-modernism. I don't understand, said my Guest. Well, I went on, I was thinking of the avant-garde movement, about the effect it had. I still don't understand, said my Guest. Well, I said, how can I put it, it was the avant-garde movement that first upset the balance, and things like that leave a mark. But this is all so vulgar, he said, we had elegance. That's what you think, I said, I don't agree, Futurism, for example, was vulgar, it celebrated noise and war, I think it had a vulgar side to it, I'll go further, there's even something slightly vulgar about your own Futurist odes. Is that why you wanted to see me?, he asked, in order to insult me. To be exact, it wasn't me who wanted to see you, I said, it was you who wanted to see me. I received a message from you, he said. That's a good one, I said, this morning I was in Azeitão sitting quietly under a tree reading, it was you who called me. All right, said my Guest, as you wish, let's not argue, let's just say I'd like to know what your intentions are. In relation to what?, I asked. In relation to me, for example, said my Guest, that's what interests me. You don't find that a little egocentric?, I asked. Of course, he replied, I am egocentric, but what do you want me to do about it, all poets are egocentric, and my ego has a very special centre, indeed if you wanted me to tell you where that centre is I couldn't. I've come up with a few hypotheses myself, I said, I've spent my life hypothesising about you and now I'm tired of it, that's what I wanted to tell you. *Please*, he said, don't abandon me to all these people who are so certain about everything, they're dreadful. You don't need me, I said, don't talk nonsense, the whole world admires you, I was the one who needed you, but now it's time to stop, that's all. Did my company displease you?, he asked. No, I said, it was very important, but it troubled me, let's just say that you had a disquieting effect on me. I know, he said, with me it always finishes that way, but don't you think that's precisely what literature should do, be disquieting I mean?, personally I don't trust literature that soothes people's consciences. Neither do I, I agreed, but you see, I'm already full of disquiet, your disquiet just adds to mine and becomes anxiety. I prefer anxiety to utter peace, he said, given the choice.

My Guest opened the wine list and read it attentively. How are you supposed to choose a wine without first having chosen your meal?, he said, this really is a bizarre restaurant. They serve almost exclusively fish dishes, I said, that's why they mostly offer white wines, but if you prefer red, there's a house red that might not be too bad. No, no, he said, tonight I'll drink white wine too, but you'll have to help me choose, I don't know the names, they're all new. Young or old?, I asked. Old, he said, I

99

don't like fizzy wines. I don't know if you've noticed but there's a Colares Chita, which is a wine from your day. My Guest approved and said: It's a wine from Azenhas do Mar, in 1923 it won a gold medal in Rio de Janeiro, I was living in Campo de Ourique at the time.

Mariazinha came over to us again and I ordered a bottle of Colares. Would you like to order your food now?, asked Mariazinha. Look, I said, if you don't mind, we'd like to drink a glass of wine first before choosing, we're thirsty and besides we want to drink a toast. That's fine by me, said Mariazinha, the kitchen's open until two and the restaurant closes at three, so feel free. He left us only to return soon after with a bottle and an ice bucket. Tonight we have a literary menu, he said as he was opening the bottle, Pedrinho chose the names, *es el apocalipse, caballeros*. Who's Pedrinho?, I asked. Pedrinho's the young fellow who advises us in the kitchen, said Mariazinha, he's terribly cultured, he did a literature course at Évora. Not someone else from the Alentejo, I said. Have you got anything against them?, asked Mariazinha with a haughty look, I'm from there too, from Estremoz. No, I've got nothing against them, I replied, it's just that my day has been full of people from the Alentejo, I've been bumping into them everywhere. We're international, said Mariazinha, with a shake of his ponytail, and left us to ourselves.

My Guest raised his glass. Let's drink a toast, he said. Right, I said, to what? To the next century, he said, you're going to need all the luck you can get, this was my century and I felt at home in it, but you might have some problems in the next one. Who's "you"?, I asked. The people alive now, he replied, you fin-de-siècle people.

We've already got masses of problems, I said, we really need a toast. I'd also like to drink to *saudosismo*,* said my Guest, raising his glass again, I miss poor old *saudosismo*, there are no *saudosistas* left, Portugal's become so very European. But you're European, I said, you're the most European writer of the twentieth century, I'm sorry, but you're the last person who should say such things. But I never left Lisbon, he said, I never left Portugal, oh, I liked Europe, but only as an idea, I sent other people off to Europe: one friend to England, another to Paris, but not me, I stayed put in my aunt's house. It was comfortable, I said, very comfortable. That's right, he went on, perhaps I've always been a bit of a coward, do you know what I mean?, but I'll tell you something, cowardice produced some of the bravest writing of the century, for example, that Czech writer who wrote in German, I can't remember his name just now, but don't you think he wrote some extraordinarily brave things? Kafka, I said, his name was Kafka. That's right, my Guest said, and yet he was a bit of a coward too. He took a sip of wine and went on: There's something cowardly about his diary, but what courage he had to write that magnificent book of his, you know, the one about guilt. *The Trial*?, I asked, is that the one you mean? Of course, he said, the most courageous book of the century, he has the courage to say that we are all guilty. Guilty of what?, I asked. I don't know, he said, of being born, perhaps, and of what happens afterwards, we're all guilty.

---

* A philosophical–political movement, mystical and nationalistic in character, founded by the poet Teixeira de Pascoaes in the first decade of the twentieth century. Its name comes from the word *saudade*, which describes the melancholic nostalgia one feels for people, things, pleasures and times now lost.

Mariazinha came over wearing a luminous smile, his powder was beginning to melt slightly in the heat, but his expression remained ingratiating. Right, *caballeros*, he said, I'm going to tell you what the menu of the day is, it's a poetic menu, but then *nouvelle cuisine* demands poetry, as a starter we have soup *Amor de Perdição* and salad *Fernão Mendes Pinto*, what do you think? The names are certainly picturesque, I said, but you'll have to explain what they mean. Right, said Mariazinha, the soup is a coriander soup made with lots of coriander and chicken giblets. The salad is an exotic mix of avocado, prawns and bean sprouts. *Am I also to blame for "nouvelle cuisine"?*, asked my Guest, *I'm not responsible for those horrible names*. No, I said, you're absolutely right, *nouvelle cuisine* is a quite separate horror. Does your friend *only* speak English?, Mariazinha interrupted, what a bore! And what do you have as a main dish?, I asked. Now let me see, said Mariazinha, we have sea bass *trágico-marítimo*,* sole *interseccionista*, Gafeira eels *à moda do Delfim* and cod *escárnio e mal-dizer*. My Guest raised one eyebrow and whispered: *Ask him how the sole is cooked*. I asked and Mariazinha looked slightly irritated. It's stuffed with ham, he said, that's why it's called *interseccionista*, because it's made from fish and meat. My Guest smiled ironically and nodded. And what about the eels *à moda do Delfim*, I asked, how are they served? They're cooked in *moira*, said Mariazinha, it's a speciality of the house. I don't know what that is, I said, can you explain? Look, said Mariazinha, you know what *caldeirada* is, a sort of fish stew, right?, well *moira* is the stock you get from the

* See Note on Recipes, page 109

caldeirada, I'll tell you how it's made, you cut the fat off the eels and add coarse salt and vinegar to it. Then this mixture, which is very tasty, is added to the stewed eels themselves, it's more or less the same as eels *à moda da Murtosa*, only more refined, that's why we call it Gafeira eels *à moda do Delfim*. But Gafeira doesn't exist, I said, it's an imaginary place, a literary place. That doesn't matter, said Mariazinha, Portugal's full of lakes, you can always find a Gafeira. I'll have that then, I said, but only a half-portion,, just to get an idea.

Mariazinha left and my Guest filled our glasses again. This place is incredible, he said. Forgive me changing the subject, I said, but I'd like you to tell me about your childhood, it really intrigues me. My childhood?, exclaimed my Guest, I've never talked to anyone about my childhood and we're not going to talk about it now at supper. Go on, I said, tell me, it's the most mysterious part of your life, this is the first and last time we'll meet, I don't want to miss the opportunity. Look, said my Guest, I had a happy childhood, really. It's true my father died, but I hardly noticed it, I found another father, he was a good, silent man, he wasn't a father exactly, more of a symbol, and it's good to live with symbols. And what about your mother?, I asked, you were very close to her, your critics, or some of them at least, even suggest you had some sort of Oedipus complex. What!, said my Guest, I had a perfectly straightforward relationship with her, my mother was a simple person, she had no concept of pretence, look, I let people think I had a mysterious childhood by completely eliminating it from my writing, but it's all nonsense, really, it was just to put the critics off the scent, they're such busybodies, and so I set traps for them beforehand. You're a liar, I said, an utter liar, you may have deceived your critics, but you're not going to deceive me as well, you're not being honest with me. Look, he said, I'm not honest in the sense you mean, the only emotions I experience are in the form of genuine pretence, I consider your kind of honesty a form of poverty, the supreme truth is to pretend, I've always believed that. You're exaggerating, I said, now you're a liar twice over, isn't that right? Yes, that's right, replied my Guest, the important thing is to feel. Exactly, I said, I was always convinced that you did in fact feel everything, indeed I always thought that you felt things normal people couldn't feel, I always believed in your occult powers, you're a sorcerer, and that's why I'm here and why I've had the day I've had. And are you pleased with the day you've had?, he asked. I don't quite know how to put it, I said, but I feel quieter, lighter. That's what you needed, he said. I'm very grateful to you, I replied.

Mariazinha arrived with the soup. It turned out to be a very traditional coriander soup, *nouvelle cuisine* had invented nothing but the name. My Guest nodded and said: I would never have thought you could eat so well in Alcântara, in my day there were no restaurants in this area at all, just cheap bars serving boiled cod. That's Europe for you, I said, the European influence. When I was alive, said my Guest, Europe was something remote, far off, it was a dream. Did you dream about it a lot?, I asked. No, he said, not much, but my friend Mário did, he dreamed about it all the time, but he suffered a terrible disenchantment, I, as you know, preferred to go to Rossio station and wait for the trains to arrive from Paris, in those days the Paris train came in at Rossio, what I liked most was reading about the journey on other people's faces. Yes, I said, you always did like to delegate. And you don't?, asked my Guest. Yes, I do it too, I replied, you're right.

The next course arrived and we began to eat. I glanced questioningly at my Guest and he responded with a neutral look. How's the sole *interseccionista?*, I asked. He shook his head. As you said about Futurism, he replied, it's a bit vulgar. But it looks good, I said. Oh, it's excellent, he said, that's what lends it its slight vulgarity.

We ate in silence. The sound of muffled music filled the room, piano music, Liszt perhaps. At least the music's good, I said. I don't like music, said my Guest, I never did. That surprises me, I said, it really does. I only like popular music, he went on, waltzes and things like that, but I do like Viana da Mota, don't you? I do, I said, he's a bit like Liszt, don't you think? Maybe, he said, but he's very Portuguese.

Mariazinha came to clear away the plates. He gave a list of desserts with bizarre-sounding names, but my Guest seemed unenthusiastic. Your friend's depressed, said Mariazinha, he looks so gloomy, poor thing, he's English, isn't he? I've already told you, I exclaimed, in a slightly irritated voice, he's Portuguese but he just happens to like speaking English. No need to get angry, *caballero*, said Mariazinha, and removed the plates.

You look tired, said my Guest, would you like to go for a little walk? I could do with some air, I said, it's been a long day, endless. I called Mariazinha over and asked for the bill. Let me pay, said my Guest. Certainly not, I protested, the restaurant was my idea, and besides I've been carefully saving my money all day just so that

I could pay for this meal, so, please, don't insist. Mariazinha blew out the candle on the table and accompanied us to the door. *Hasta la vista, caballeros*, he said, *gracias y buenas noches. Goodbye, sir*, said my Guest.

We crossed the road and walked past the harbour station. I'm going to walk as far as the end of the quay, said my Guest, won't you come with me? Of course I will, I said. By the door to the harbour station was a beggar, with an accordion round his neck. When he saw us, he held out his hand and recited some incomprehensible litany of complaints. At the end of it all he murmured: God bless you, gentlemen, can you spare any change? My Guest stopped and thrust his hand into his pocket, pulled out his wallet and removed an ancient note. I've only got old money, he said, looking concerned, perhaps you can help me out. I felt in my pocket and pulled out a one hundred *escudo* note. It's all the money I have left, I said, I'm cleaned out, but it's a nice note, don't you think? He looked at it and smiled. He held out the note to the Accordionist and asked: Do you know any of the old songs? I know "Old Lisbon", said the Accordionist eagerly, I know all the *fados*. No, older than that, said my Guest, something from the 1930s, you must remember, you're not a young man yourself. I might know it, said the Accordionist, tell me what you'd like to hear. How about "Your eyes are so lovely"?, said my Guest. Oh, I know that one, said the Accordionist happily, I know it very well. My Guest handed him the hundred *escudo* note and said: Walk a few yards behind us will you, and play that tune for us, but quietly because we have to talk. He assumed a confidential air and whispered in my ear: I once danced to this tune with my girlfriend, but no one knows that. You used to dance?, I exclaimed, I would never have thought it. I was an excellent dancer, he said, I taught myself from a little book called *The Modern Dancer*, I always liked books like that, ones that taught you how to do things, I used to practise at night when I got home from work, I used to dance on my own and write poems and letters to my girlfriend. You were really fond of her, I said. She was the clockwork train of my heart, he replied. He stopped walking and made me stop too. The Accordionist stopped as well, but went on playing. Look at the moon, said my Guest, it's the same moon my girlfriend and I used to look up at when we went for a stroll to Poço do Bispo, isn't that odd?

We'd reached the end of the quay. Right, he said, we met on this bench and we'll say goodbye on this bench, you must be tired, you can tell the old man to go away now. He sat down and I went to tell the Accordionist that we no longer needed his music. The old man wished me good night. I turned round and only then did I realise that my Guest had vanished.

The garden was plunged in silence, a cool breeze had got up, it caressed the mulberry leaves. Good night, I said, or rather, goodbye. Who or what was I saying goodbye to? I didn't really know, but that was what I felt like saying, out loud. Goodbye and goodnight to you all, I said again. Then I leaned my head back and looked up at the moon.

A NOTE ON RECIPES
IN THIS BOOK

page 27   *Feijoada* is a bean soup or stew – each region of Portugal has its own variety – embodying a lavish selection of meats (pork being obligatory), sausage and vegetables.

36   *Reguengos de Monsaraz* is a well-known red wine from the region of that name in the Lower Alentejo.

37–8 *Sarrabulho à moda do Douro*, a rich dish from the North, which requires no description as Senhor Casimiro's Wife provides the recipe.

40   *Papos de anjos de Mirandela* (angels' double chins) are little confections of egg and almond, originating in the convents.

47   *Migas*, *açorda* and *sargalheta* are specialities of the Alentejo region. *Migas*, as the plural form of the word suggests, come in many forms: the basis is always constituted by homebaked bread allowed to go stale, then cooked over the fire with a little fat until it is reduced to a fried and dried sort of pulp which can serve as an accompaniment to meat or fish.

Açorda is a pulp made out of homebaked bread allowed to go stale and generally flavoured with garlic and *coentros* (fresh coriander leaves). It may serve to accompany meat or fish, or as the basis of more complicated recipes. The best-known variation is *açorda de mariscos* as mentioned on page 78, in which the pulp is flavoured with shrimp and other seafood and bound with fresh egg.

Sargalheta is a winter soup made of bacon, sausage, egg, potato and onion.

55   Pineapple (or orange) *sumol* is a fizzy drink flavoured with the fruit in question and very sweet.

59   "Janelas Verdes' Dream", the creation of the Barman at the Museum of Ancient Art (and thus of the author), derives its name from the Museum's also being known as the Museum "das Janelas Verdes" (of the Green Windows), from the name of the street in which it is located.

78   *Arroz de tamboril* is rice cooked with monkfish, tomato, garlic and coriander leaves, served on the boil at the table in the pot in which it is cooked.

78   *Açorda de mariscos* is described in the note to page 47.

78   The *sopa alentejana* here discussed is supposed to be the simplest cuisine of the region – a cuisine based, like all the recipes of the poor, on few and simple ingredients (in this case, boiling salted water, toasted garlic bread, fresh coriander leaves and raw eggs), but abundant in soups of all kinds.

83   *Ensopada de borreguinho à moda de Borba*, an Alentejo speciality, is a stew of lamb's flesh and offal flavoured with vinegar and served on thin slices of bread that thus turn into broth.

83   *Poejada* is a soup of stale bread, garlic, onion and fresh cheese, flavoured with *poejos* (a sort of wild mint).

100   Colares, near Sintra, is famous for its exquisite white wine.

102   As with every menu of "creative cookery" or *nouvelle cuisine*, that of Mariazinha – who has worked in a *pousada*, a State-run luxury hotel, often a converted castle, villa or convent, like the Spanish *paradores* – is entirely the product of fantasy. But as it is a "literary" menu it is worth clarifying the references:

Amor de Perdição is the title of the most famous novel (1863) by Camilo Castelo Branco, a great writer of the Romantic era. Fernão Mendes Pinto (*c.* 1510–83), navigator and adventurer, lived mostly in the Far East and wrote the *Peregrinação*, a sort of grandiose epic poem in prose. Still in the area of seaborne adventure is the *História trágico-marítima*, a miscellany ascribed to various authors, giving the accounts of sixteenth- and seventeenth-century shipwreck-survivors. "Interseccionismo" was an artistic movement founded by Fernando Pessoa in 1914 with the publication of his poem "Chuva oblíqua" ("Slanting rain"). The "Cantigas de escárnio e mal-dizer" ("Lays of slander and disdain"), are the satirical, comic-realistic form of the Galician-Portuguese lyric tradition between the late twelfth and early fourteenth centuries. As for the lake at Gafeira, it is a fantasy location in which José Cardoso Pires sets his novel *O Delfim* (1968). The recipe for *enguias da Gafeira à moda do "Delfim"* happily coincides with the traditional recipe for *enguias à moda da Murtosa* and is described in the text.

SERGIO VECCHIO